IN DEFEN(

In Defence of Pseudoscience

Reflex Fiction Volume Five

REFLEX PRESS

First published as a collection in 2022 by Reflex Press
Abingdon, Oxfordshire, OX14 3SY
www.reflex.press

A CIP catalogue record of this book is
available from the British Library.

ISBN: 978-1-914114-13-7

1 3 5 7 9 10 8 6 4 2

Printed and bound in Great Britain by
Severn, Gloucester.

Cover image by B.erne

www.reflex.press/in-defence-of-pseudoscience/

CONTENTS

Synonym for Tree on Fire
Becca Yenser
SPRING 2021 FIRST PLACE

Lately you find feathers in the snow: downy, juvenile. You find bones in your salmon and hair in your mouth.

The last time you touched another human being was five months ago, unless you count the gynecologist who warned you the gel would be warm. *Warm*, you said, *warm?* You didn't quite cry but looked off into the distance while Garth Brooks nearly cried, too.

Underneath the snow, a sad garden of pill bug exoskeletons and the tomato plant who tried all summer to produce, despite the light-socket heat every day, who finally, in August, grew one tiny misshapen tomato with scars and a glossy green bottom. Everyone is trying.

The blood that comes out of you is a black web, and you are almost impressed by its intuitive precision for horror; this isn't the Barbie-pink spotting of pregnancy. There's nothing cute about it.

Your ex brings kimchi that explodes in your fridge. You eat it anyway, later finding the hole in the glass where the acid ate it away. Everyone is eating.

When you see your uterus on the computer screen, you think, *That's it?* You once felt so full of life you would explode, the baby opening and closing its fists until it didn't.

You hold the bones of your grief against snow against blood against feathers against glass against scars against heat. You are alone on a golf course in the snow, and a single tree is on fire.

Wittgenstein Sits at the Piano After the Long Cacophony of the War and Contemplates Past, Present, Future, Love, Loss, Obsession, Poise, Determination, Pain, Denial, Anger, Bargaining, Acceptance and Everything Else Wrapped Within the Meaning of 'Can't'

Matt Kendrick

SPRING 2021 SECOND PLACE

The notes sound in his head. Five of them. The first ones he played as a boy, legs dangling like crotchet stems beneath him. He reaches forwards with his left hand, slows, pauses, pulls back. His hand falls heavy in his lap.

The second try, he rests his fingers on the keys and is shocked by the veil of dust, the cold, unfamiliar feel of the wood, the black keys' hard edges. When his legs were finally long enough to reach the pedals, he told Mutti the piano was as much a part of him as an arm or a lung. He laughs at that. A bitter laugh. Mourns for the young man at his grand debut whose storm-surge cadenza forecast concerts and concerts and concerts...

Then the gunshot, the stretcher, the field medic's tent, the leather strip between his teeth. In his inside jacket pocket, he has Mutti's letter in which she asked, What will you do? She meant, Now that you can't tie your laces, can't write your name, can't play the simplest of children's preliminary etudes.

His throat is a parched riverbed.

He smashes the heel of his left hand into the keys one, two, three, four, five times over.

The echo is more than the notes. It is early morning scales slipping into sight-reading, memorising, meandering improvisations, mud-slumped memories of war.

He breathes.

He closes his eyes.

He imagines a thread pulling straight his spine, imagines the bridge of separation between the piano and himself mending like knitted flesh over an open wound, an audience, their top hats and tiaras – they are crowding forwards – and he starts to play, sketches an idea, a chromatic progression that burbles upwards in quavers and semiquavers and semidemiquavers, a second line interwoven with the first, with trills and grace notes, all quickening and crescendoing, twisting, cascading, until his fingers, four fingers and a thumb, are

rapid white-water rippling so fast across the keys that it is difficult –
no, it is impossible – in the precise moment of watching him, to know
whether he has two hands or one.

Water Spells
Evelyn Forest
SPRING 2021 THIRD PLACE

I lay on my back and watched stars wheeling while the waves carried me as kindred salt. In those days, I hoped for nothing more than buoyancy while I polished the inside of a shell.

Floating like this and forgetting, I circled the world three times. Immune to the accidental shift of hemispheres and failing to count the passing seasons, I washed up on the shores of a new continent thinking I had come home. I walked into a familiar house, only to find everything reversed and made into its opposite. I reached out to trace the edges of the room, but my hand sank into surfaces as if they were pools and lakes. I dipped my cup in a puddle glittering with moonlight and sipped the earthy flavours, my tongue alert for mercury.

Then ambling into that imposter kitchen came a stranger. He picked out one sharp memory and blunted it in his hands until it became a tool for new dinners, something that spreads butter or opens a jar of sweet jam, undoing the painful separation of glass. In that sudden opening, everything that couldn't be said began to flow through me again, only to instantly evaporate with the heat of my skin touching his. My eyes gathered in their wet corners the memory of shapes and colours, then his touch wiped away the past as if its only purpose was to bring me to this moment. Poetry became history.

In the presence of this magician, I waited to see what else was up his sleeve. A flurry of doves burst from his pocket. Confused by their wings, I stepped back, and he caught my elbow. Then watching my face, he unwound from between us a mile of silk scarves in streams of blue and purple and emerald green, as if infinity belonged to him. The room tilted, and I was floating again, lost in the sensation of his hand on my hip, on my cheek, on the knives of my kitchen.

Yet somehow, we were also still feasting at the summer table, and sunlight was slanting through flowers, falling warm onto my bare feet.

Behind the Scenes
Nora Nadjarian
SPRING 2021 FOURTH PLACE

The zoo keeper walks into the cage. The zoo keeper strokes tiger fur. The zoo keeper has a lot on his mind. The zoo keeper talks to the animals. The zoo keeper laughs at the spider monkey, and the spider monkey laughs back. The zoo keeper visits the aardvarks every evening. The zoo keeper has his face licked by the lion. The zoo keeper calls his wife and says he'll be late. The zoo keeper notices the macaw is losing its feathers. The zoo keeper mucks out the gorilla cage. The zoo keeper thinks of ways to entertain lemurs. The zoo keeper carries buckets of dead meat and bones. The zoo keeper thinks of the colour of blood. The zoo keeper watches the leopard rip an antelope, crack its ribs. The zoo keeper thinks of body inside body inside body inside body. The zoo keeper looks at his gloves and their dark stains. The zoo keeper remembers his son's head emerging. The zoo keeper thinks of birth and death. The zoo keeper knows that humans maul humans. The zoo keeper keeps sane. The zoo keeper keeps count. The zoo keeper opens up all the cages and waits.

Down by the Shore on a Summer's Day
Joanne Clague

When my dog presses his nose to the window, he can smell the sand in the glass. When he perks his ears, he's listening to the tiny pebbles tumbling over each other beneath the waves. And when he rests his chin on my thigh he gazes at me as if the sluggish blood in my veins has all the force of a tsunami.

I summon the strength to direct my gaze at the sensor bar. Words appear on the screen, and she peers at them.

Her mouth turns down when she asks, 'Are you joking?'

Then she says, 'Are you serious?' Now she's laughing.

When I twitch one eyebrow, my dog hears a belly laugh and barks in joy.

An elaborate plan is made, and I'm encased in metal and motors. I pretend I am the soft parts of a crab protected by its shell. We go on our final adventure to the magical line where the land meets the water. My dog stalks the oyster-catchers who strut about officiously, always just out of reach.

My eyelids are heavy, so I allow them to drop. I imagine stretching my arms over my head and then reaching down to take off my shoes and the socks she unrolled over my useless feet this morning. There is no cage in my mind, and I am free to rise, to stand on the lip of the foaming tide, bare toes nibbled by swirling water that gently washes the sand from under the soles of my feet, grain by grain.

I open my eyes when my dog presses his nose into the palm of my limp hand. In the heat-haze, a round-bellied infant squeezes seaweed in his fists, and his laugh unfurls like a string of pearls over the waves.

Geyserville, CA, 2019
Noemi Scheiring-Olah

It's never dark anymore.

The sky moans in rust. The air scratches. And I'm still awake in bed when Mom opens the door of my room, 'We're leaving.'

I get up, put on a thin, pale-blue nightgown, and crouch to pull out a plastic suitcase from under my bed. Swirling dust makes me cough.

We've practiced this before. Clothes. Toiletries. Chargers. Laptop. Phone. Headphones. School stuff. Done. Execution mode. Just like Mom.

The suitcase's four wheels roll on the dread-pale planks.

I stop.

Did I forget something?

No.

I *heard* something.

Sheep-shap.

Whistling?

Sheep-shap, sheep-sheep-shap.

Is it a... *bird*?

I can't remember the last time I heard birds. There is only cracking, snapping, prickling heat.

Sheep-shap.

I release the suitcase's handle and turn back. Orange mist everywhere. And... *Sheep-shap.*

I rush to my soot-powdered chest of drawers and kneel, yanking out the bottom drawer. *Sheep-shap, sheep-shap* gets louder.

Lost pairs of ankle socks, gold star stickers, friendship bracelets, pieces of yellow Lego fly out as I search for the bird inside.

'Fuck's sake.' Mom's behind me. 'We've been through this.'

My hands scour the drawer, 'Can't you hear the bird?'

'We have to leave. *Now!*'

And I find it. A small, carved wooden bird, long tail and short beak glisten with brown varnish.

I smile at it. Grandma bought it for me at a DIY fair years ago, where she was selling baskets. I always wanted her to teach me to weave, but...

When I asked Mom if she could make baskets too, she said, 'I make money.'

I cup the bird in my palms.

Mom grabs my arm. Hard. Her fright travels into me like electricity.

I jump up, holding the bird against my chest.

Sheep-shap, it says, snuggling up to my collarbone.

Mom pulls me away from the drawer and drops my arm on the pulled-out handle of the suitcase.

'Let's go.' Her voice is even.

Before getting in the SUV, Mom and I stop at both sides of the open car doors and look back at the house.

Home.

The bird stirs in my palm.

In Defence of Pseudoscience
Barclay Rafferty

Iris cupped the yellowhammer, tangled it in dog-rose, pressed her thumbs to its chest. I pretended not to hear the breastbone squelch. 'Scientists don't like the word *pseudoscience*,' I said. 'A media sound-bite. You either prove an invention works, or you don't. You offer evidence or spout untestable claims – about birds wrapped in flowers, elixirs of life, etc.'

Iris drowned the thud of the yellowhammer with prayers, incantations to Green Jesus. The ruffled corpse anchored itself in the tussocky grass, under blackthorn shoots sprinkled white with eggs. The parapet was too high for Iris's arms to feign magic, make a passerine bird disappear. Overwinter survival rates had plummeted, we were told, and the song-post was silent that morning.

The hedgerow was more than just a boundary or property demarcation. It screened us from office blocks, unsightly factories. A wildlife corridor, it protected cattle, crops, stopped the ocean winds swooping in and doing God knows what, picking us up and carrying us out to sea.

'I hate nature,' Iris said, tracing the face of a pound coin: rose, thistle, shamrock, leek. A new one each day over Easter. 'Heads he'll have flown off by morning.'

It was heads. And we never talked about it again.

~

Iris didn't say a word, but I knew her footfall.

She tossed Converse to the soil where I buried the yellowhammer, danced, soles jet as coffin-bottom dirt, did that one foot to the other sway, roboted through homebound schoolchildren. One wore a lemony scarf over her beak, wiped sweat clean from her brow.

'We should give your cloud-seeding experiment another go,' Iris said, popping blitz-black berries beneath her toes. She talked about a recurring dream she had about luminous things haunting her night season, a phrase she learnt from *The Book of Common Prayer*. I didn't want to ask about newfound faith, made a shit joke about chemistry never changing instead. 'Without pseudoscience,' she said, 'there wouldn't be two thirty-somethings, dancing.'

We smoked in the spot where once we'd reanimated dead birds, watched horseshoe bats catch crane flies on outstretched wings. Just two vampires in springtime, higher than Dracula's cheekbones, sink-ing deeper into the gossamer.

Lucky Day
Patricia Q Bidar

I'm a lucky bastard of scattered habits. My books marked by ladies' underthings. They bring me tea and flowers and leave earrings in my bedclothes.

She is the best of them. Honey hair and citrine eyes I daren't meet. At eight in the morning, I awake in a jumble of sheets. Slip out in the nick of time. Husbandly shouts emit like brass notes from between window rails. The scent of her is still on my hands.

At ten o'clock, I hear from friends: she's divorced. If I have something to do with that, no one but honey-headed her could connect the dots. We are immaculate.

I hear she's fled: Ibiza. At noon I carry on in gray Astoria, under the 1964 bridge to Washington. By two, I'm in Rock Springs, Wyoming. Riding to the trona mines with dirty-necked men in a busted down truck.

Four p.m. finds me on the downswing, an ordinary rector at a Rust Belt house of prayer. When I finish, the pews shine amber.

By six, I'm running sound at the Fort Worth opera house. When the lights dim, I feel a tug on my laces. I know not to meet those olive-lemon eyes. She extends an invitation in Catalan. In a low postscript, she calls me a fraudulent work of art.

She performs her warbling singthing to wild acclaim. But before the curtain, she's gone. I rise from my soundboard and fall to my knees. My knotted-together laces piledrive me to carpet. I loosen my tie and reach for my comb.

Ten p.m. finds me walking the highway, graceless and bleary. Music caroms in my head. A black splash strikes my legs. Her and those eyes: that lethal duo. I meet citrine and come to rest without misgiving.

I awake at midnight, alone. Beyond the floating drape splays Lake Pontchartrain, that talismanic ten-mile bridge. It would appear my luck is gone. I'm unensnared; face down in estuary mud.

Double Bass, Coffin Case
Lucy Grace

I could imagine him drawing a bow languidly across thickening strings, so me and the whisky believed him. His eyes were as deep as the notes, but I could not understand his seesawing language – the vowels were different. In the hotel lift, thin fingers played homesick notes on my spine, and I was smitten. There were certainly other girls in other cities, but here in this afternoon before the concert we lay naked, pulling an extra day from the short week.

We did not talk.

When he cleaned his teeth, he stood slightly bow-legged, as though expecting his instrument.

We did not fuck.

The case stood in the corner of the room like a stopped clock; we moved warily around it. He opened it when I closed the bathroom door; we were never together. I heard the lock click and the dry rasp of his gaze running silently up and down the polished length, and knew I was not important. I did not tell him he was important to me.

He was in the bathroom when the front desk rang to say they were loading all instruments for the next leg of the tour. I quickly opened the case and I opened the wardrobe and I stood his first wooden love between complimentary white bathrobes, naked.

In the humming corridor, I laid the empty case softly onto the snakes-head carpet and climbed inside into velvety dark, softly closing the lid before he opened the door.

'How will you love now?' I wondered.

Harvest
Nkone Chaka

The wind whispers through the cornfield. It is a loose tickle beneath my upturned feet. On my back, hands buried deep into the mud by my hips, I can hear the corn speak. It too is a soft whisper. My mother does not believe that I talk to the trees and other things that grow from the ground. Sometimes, their voices are strong and fully-fledged, solid like the earth beneath my back. Other times, they are harried, dry, desperate, and drained. They tell me that they miss the rain.

My grandmother is perched atop a metal carriage pulled by an old van, hand covering her face to shield her eyes from the sun.

'It's calling me,' I tell her as I pull myself up out of the soil.

'Pulane, Pulane,' the corn hums in my ears.

'Listen. It's calling me,' I say. She pats my head and climbs down from the carriage, waving the driver over. Another van pulls up beside us. She points to a row of stalks, and both drivers smile at me as they follow her finger to the far end of the field.

'Pulane, Pulane,' the corn continues, voice full now in the early morning. I close my eyes. My grandmother's footsteps are heavy thuds as her boots sink into the mud.

'Pulane!' This time, it is a scream. *'Pulane! Pulane! Pulane!'* My eyes fly open and my head spins around to where my grandmother begins to pull the corn from its stalk. *'Pulane!'* My breath is stuck in my throat, and my legs drive themselves to where she stands, pulling and pulling.

'Stop!' I cry, reaching out to her. 'Stop! What are you doing? Stop!' My chest is full with the effort of shouting, and the corn's cry makes my ears bleed. My hands shake as I fight to pull my grandmother's hands away. For a moment, she is puzzled, head tilted to the side as she watches me struggle, and then her face changes, surprise becoming a disappointed frown. I am soft, she realizes. I am her daughter's daughter. She pulls and picks as the corn continues to scream.

I Sit at Home and Wait for Passive Vengeance
Cate Sweeney

They arrive, the friends, same-sex couple, female. I recognise them, though don't know them. He takes their coats. They haven't dressed up. Like they'd all forgotten how, or their clothes don't fit anymore.

And I know.

One wears an oversized Aran jumper, baggy, bobbly, sleeves pushed up, a jumper that's meant to hide something: anorexia, extra weight, or maybe a pregnancy. The other one stands behind her, dark, like a shadow.

And I know, and he doesn't know I know.

Aran hands over a potted hyacinth, budding, brazen in its purple potential. They open arms, pause, for a hug, like they'd all forgotten how and need permission. An awkward little laugh.

'G and Ts? Wine?'

'Just tonic for me,' says Aran.

He moves toward where I'm standing in the open plan kitchen, says, nibbles ready, darling. Touches me on the arm, a little validation, like leftovers.

I smile as I hate him. And he doesn't know.

'Alexa?' he shouts.

Alexa flashes, ever obedient. 'Play Ibiza Chillout,' and the music begins unwinding, raindrops on bongoes, twinkling chimes, a synth suggests and fades to a sigh.

'Reminds us of the good old days, eh?'

Alexa knows too, but he doesn't know we know.

I walk round with my canapés, but they don't notice me. They're entranced by themselves on the giant TV screen: life-size photos of Ibiza trips, dates helpfully displayed, courtesy of Alexa.

'I can't believe that's ten years ago,' says Aran.

Still more photos of them, in bikinis, swim shorts, spray foam, gathering round bulbous jugs of Sangria, gleaming and red, raising their glasses. What fun we all had!

Then more recent photos begin. Just us two. Sensible in cities: Budapest, Prague, Paris, Bruges. Happy as anoraks in the rain.

Yet, I feel his alarm build, sense his skin prickling across the room as the montage continues ever more present, until a series of shots of tangled naked limbs.

'Alexa, stop! I said stop!' he says.

And she does; the current photo freezes, the date, a few months ago.

And now we all know.

Ad Nauseam
Alice Rogers

Nuclear summertime, 1967, and the air is thick with insects. Biting you down to muscle and bone, drawing blood until you're woozy with it. Or maybe that's the hunger, the exhaustion, the sleeplessness. But ain't it easier to blame something you can swat with your hand?

SMACK. The sound of our war. Soupy hot orange air, like boiled Tang. Jay's got a sachet of the powdered stuff in his clutch belt that he thinks nobody knows about. I swill iodine-tinged water through my teeth and think about it: stealing it when Jay sleeps.

We barely sleep. I'll never get that fucking Tang.

Late afternoon, a finger of sunlight slides over my face; wiggled through a crack in the dense canopy overhead. I know it because I saw it coming, sliding over the bobbing row of helmets in front of me, the same way a priest presses holy water between an infant's eyes.

Then it hits me. I close my eyes. The world slows, narrows. I forget about war and mosquitos, both fat with my blood. I forget about Tang, about the way my tongue is sticking to the roof of my mouth with thirst. All I know is the slip of sunlight over me. Diffuse, sticky. Orange like an egg yolk, fuck the Tang. Glossy and spitting in the pan. First thing I'm gonna do when I get home is crack an egg in some oil, so hot the edges get all feathery and brown—

The light moves on to the guy behind, and I open my eyes to humid dripping jungle. To the long, snaking line of men in which I'm a single, solitary scale. No matter how many times I try to blink it away, it's always there waiting. The shadowy path through the trees, the wall of jungle bristling with things that want me dead. Sweat stinging something awful in the crop of mosquito bites bristling on the nape of my neck, bites that I can't stop scratching raw.

Another slice of light passes over me. And I think, *this time*, as I screw my eyes shut.

What is it again that they say about madness?

Ronnie Boils an Egg
Jupiter Jones

His name escapes her. He said sex began in 1963, or '67? The year is moot, but he was right, in a way, it didn't exist before, *before*. What was his name? Some sort of librarian, from Hull of all places. Not the man she had had sex with once, oh, God, no! The librarian. She'd never been to Hull.

The pan of water comes to the boil, surface erupting sporadically. Ronnie balances an egg on her long-handled spoon – pauses – but no, his name drifts past in the steam. She lowers the egg, watching for cracks, her smoker's mouth pursed like a cat's arse. Up-ends her three-minute timer, limps to the table, unfurls yesterday's paper, glances at bad-news headlines, turns to the obits.

Every morning, she looks for the man she had sex with, once.

'Still not dead, old bastard.'

Aloud, her voice is croaky from cigarettes, rusty from living alone.

Sand races through the timer's isthmus. She fetches a tarnished silver teaspoon. And salt. She extinguishes the gas flame.

Ronnie eats the egg.

Scooping out the lightly boiled albumen, savouring slippery solidity between her tongue and the roof of her mouth, she turns the shell over, stoves-in the skull-like dome; confound the witches. Let them find some other mode of transport. Reaching for a teacloth printed with a faded image of Santiago de Compostela, she rubs at a dribble of yolk congealing on her dress. It leaves a mark. It always does.

She takes the pan and eggcup to the sink; the tap has one of those rubber end-spouts. The rubber perished long since. The water is cold. Forty years in London, and she still feels cold; her bones creak in the damp. She misses the sun, the sea, misses the – Larkin. That was it.

Craft Coffee and Climate Change
Stella Klein

Today, as we queue for coffee, as we move along the line of marble cake and burnished custard tarts, ears plugged to our separate beats, outside a north-easterly squall snaps branches and awnings, sends cartons dancing along the pavement.

Yesterday, elsewhere, there was flooding. Here in the city, just swollen banks and swirling drains, slender moats of plate-glass and shimmering steel. Rivers ran along the pavements, down corporate steps and slopes towards the tube station. The cleaners spent all day in entrances swishing brooms towards the brimming canal.

Last summer, elsewhere, it was raging fires; the flare and crackle of ancient wood, thick billows of smoke across quivering skies. We saw it up there on the muted screen as we waited to be served: jets of water pounding at blackened trees; then took to our corners to sip our frappés through plastic straws, suck on crushed ice, and think about the death of insects.

At the front of the line, our same baristas smile, shout our orders. We pay contactless, draw out our loyalty cards and unplug our ears to the reverberations of café chic: the chink of cups, the hiss of steam, the lull of a folksy love song; which is all we need right now.

Your Home Town
Patricia Q Bidar

*During pregnancy, cells from the fetus cross the placenta and enter the
mother's body, where they can become part of her tissues.*

Rounded hills overlook the low town that birthed you. Daytime
is the crack of little league bats. The Wednesday 'fish wrapper' de-
livered by a towheaded neighbor. The discount bakery and the smell
of hot white bread. Your father works long hours as a butcher. From
the bedroom window, you and your sisters can see the green-blue
Vincent Thomas Bridge, leading to the Terminal Island canneries and
the women's prison. Your aunt leaves her spinster's studio to super-
vise you girls while your mother does her time.

*This cellular invasion means that mothers carry unique genetic ma-
terial from their children's bodies, creating what biologists call a mi-
crochimera, named for the legendary beasts made of different animals.*

Eastward squat the pumpkinlike tanks of the Los Angeles refinery.
At night, its spires are magic: emitting dragon breath plumes. The
scene is gold lit at night.

A whale skeleton is discovered embedded within the refinery
grounds. Dubbed Raquel because her bones are 'well-stacked.' Your
aunt drags you sisters to the excavation site. She sells cans of Bubble
Up and Dr Pepper from a folding chair, exchanging ribald jokes with
the diggers and their assistants. You and your sisters climb the refinery's metal staircases with boys from Wilmington and Harbor City.
Your mother stays gone.

*CHIMERA: a fire-breathing monster, which, according to the
Homeric poems, was of divine origin. She was brought up by
Amisodarus, king of Caria, and afterwards made great havoc in all the
country around and among men.*

In the night's soul middle, foghorns and the train spread their
sonic balm. You sisters have scattered across the land. Been loved by
a thousand men. Part of you remains, embedded in the town's tissue,
adrift in its petroleum perfume.

Kind of Regal
D B Miller

The only place for her to sit was on a freestanding lawn chair in the back of his dented car. Moncef broke a sweat trying to secure it with the help of three ropes, a broken seat belt and the two Mohammeds from reception. This wasn't what she had in mind when he offered to take her up to Tunis, but when she crawled in, feeling all eyes on her rear, she had to admit it was kind of regal.

On the highway, they chugged up the right lane with the windows open. Moncef caught her eye in the rearview and shouted over the honks of passing trucks. 'They think they're gazelles now, but when we're all sitting in the same traffic, who will be the gazelle then?'

She leaned further back, straining to catch a shock of sea between the dirty buildings. Moncef jerked the radio dial back and forth, rolling over sparks of static and something like language. On the third pass, he locked into a song and blasted the volume.

'Tell me you don't know this song!'

'I don't know this song!' she yelled back, wary of the slurred, alien scale.

'You don't know Fairuz?' The chair lurched as he hit the brakes. 'Maybe your ex was right.'

She rolled her eyes while he cackled over the drone of slowing engines. She tried to hear the music, but the plaintive voice slipped through the tinny speakers and out into the haze.

'Fairuz is a legend – a queen, really. And she was the favorite of my one true love.'

'You were married?'

'By some standards, yes,' he said, grinding the gears. 'She was bright and relatively quick on the uptake, like you. But she knew Fairuz.'

You Fold Yourself into Tiny Spaces
F C Malby

You fold yourself into tiny spaces, words come at you like rain. You tuck in your arms and feet – soles digging into your calves – so that the words don't slice your limbs. You hide your competition win in case it's seen as an indulgence, like the cakes you get for afternoon tea: miniature, crustless cucumber sandwiches, cakes and scones with clotted cream and strawberry jam. Saliva lines your lips as you imagine this.

You squeeze your words into shorter sentences and, sometimes, single words. Your arms sting with the folding and the tucking. The tiny spaces make her feel bigger, less threatened; more. You listen hard and speak less, reaching a point where the bird flying overhead, beyond the skylights, provides the distraction you need.

'Why didn't you tell me?' she asks, but you know you can't give a proper answer.

'I forgot,' you say and take a swig of hot tea, the mug leaving a ring on the mat. This will be noted.

'It sounds interesting. I'd like to read it sometime.' But the word 'interesting' sounds forced, and the 'sometime' is also *not now, later, never*. You won't know. You will be kept hanging. The words sound good, unless you can see the undertones – the seagull ripping flesh from a carcass on the edge of the shore, as it pecks and devours, turning occasionally to see if anyone is watching, picking up each foot as the tide comes in; pecks again, preens its feathers. The carcass lies motionless, ribs exposed, flesh torn away, immobilised. It's not a pretty sight, and no one sees. A passerby may find bones and bits of tendon, or an organ, or part of a limb, but it will be paralysed.

'More tea?' she asks.

'No, thank you,' you say, but she is already making the next cup.

You sew yourself back up so that nothing is exposed and it all looks pristine. The seagull flies away, but your insides still feel the rips and tears. Passers-by look at your feathers and smile. You tuck in your wings and stand up tall.

Above All Bones
Raluca Comanelea

Judy's eyes beheld the vertical, upside-down statue of Oscar Wilde resting at Père Lachaise, Parisian cemetery which holds vast quantities of bones. She was looking for Hank's hat, and she found it among those solemn graves covered in moss. Green is life. And green is also death. A simplest '*À Ma Mère*' engraved on a tombstone is breathless.

Green was the taste of that hollowed-out cigar filled with pure hash. Judy sucked it dry in an ultimate effort to embrace the secrets of the dead. Her mother told her that she was born on November 1st, a little after midnight, after having survived in a glass of water for the last months. Her night is special. Americans celebrate with masks and characters from all walks of magic: mysterious French maids, bunnies with hidden intentions, deconstructed Disney creatures. During the same night, Mexicans and Germans remember the spirits of the dead ones, ghosts who roam their streets unapologetically, invisible to the eyes of the ill. Ill with TV and liquor consumption, ill with the obsessive preoccupation of what to eat next.

Judy took a nap next to the '*À Ma Mère*' muted sign. She dreamed of being La Bella Donna, in whose name Oscar's lips have forgotten how to sing a melody. She dreamed of being the Star-Child who was said to bring pain into God's world. The most elegant cat walked by and startled Judy, forcing her back to a solemn reality, interrupting her deep affairs with Victorian literature. Judy left before dusk settled in above all bones.

Hank waited for her at the main gate on Rue de Repos. He bought her a yellow mirror reflecting a lovely Parisian café scene. Now it's broken. Hank and Judy saw a most ugly dog under the Eiffel Tower. Judy felt sorry for his ugliness. Hank didn't. Time and again, Judy feels sorry for all things ugly: women's dresses, cakey makeup on a porcelain white woman, platinum blonde dyes, chlorine-bathed chicken carcasses hung upside down.

They returned to Hotel Josephine without holding hands. Hank breathed in her ear and locked her heart on a wall overlooking The Seine.

The Wind on Mars
Kate O'Grady

We listened in the kitchen, on the wonky, failing laptop, bleary-eyed and drinking tea. The soft wail of it sounded much like our wind on earth, but lonelier, more forlorn.

'It's the sound of longing,' I said.

We held hands and glanced at each other, then back at the screen, to the still image of a fabulous titanium creature with giant parasol wings and tiny yellow feet. This structure, part bird, part machine, was called Insight. Situated two hundred and twenty-five million kilometers away, it was transmitting the sound of another world.

'I'm in awe,' I said, and you laughed.

'I'm full of wonder,' you said, and I moved my chair closer to yours.

Awe and wonder and laughter had been missing from our home for many months. Not since we had listened to the fast, steady rhythm of her heartbeat on a small handheld device in a large downtown clinic. Giddy with joy, we had not reckoned with how quickly things can change.

We lay down side-by-side on the kitchen floor, our fingers entwined, our eyes closed. We listened to the sighs of the wind on Mars and pictured the fine red dust rising on the distant planet. We imagined the wind blowing through the Martian canyons and lake beds and craters, moving and shifting and rearranging everything in its path.

The Things They Took Away
Jonathan Cardew

We owed money to men, so men came to take our things.

They took the TV.

They took the computer.

They took the stove, my boxed LEGO collection, the sofas.

They took our take-away.

One man waved a photo.

Who's this? he said.

My dad, I said.

Where is he?

Heaven.

He shrugged, scrunched it in his back pocket.

They took the cat, hamster, lampshades, rug, kettle, pots, pans, knives, forks, and egg separator.

One man unhung our mountain photos from the living room. He got a tiny hammer from his pocket and pinged out the nails.

There, he said. That's done.

They took six eggs from the fridge, leaving one.

And then they took the fridge.

Mum leaned into her whisky, watching the show. She laughed at the men. Hissed at them. Kicked her hip out whenever one walked by. They were seven. Tall and short. Fat and thin. One had a cauliflower ear. Another smiled all the time.

Doesn't matter, mum whispered, sipping her drink. Doesn't matter.

They took the doors, the curtain rails, the plug sockets.

Took the light bulbs and smoke detector.

Took the windows by smashing them out.

Mum howled.

It's so clean! she screamed. So airy!

As they were leaving, I ran up to the man who took the photo. I pointed to his pocket, the lump at his rear.

He's not really dead, I said. He left us.

Oh?

He left us and he didn't take anything.

The man pulled out the photo, smoothed it out. My dad's eyes drooped at the corners where the creases were.

He looks like you, he said.

Don't you mean I look like him?

That's what I meant, he said. Of course, that's what I meant.

And then he was gone.

More than an Itch
Emma Phillips

It was more than an itch. She felt them stirring between her shoulder blades, hard stumps at first, before the promise of feathers. She walked the hills, studied a buzzard in flight, learned to hold her breath and creep up close just to catch the moment when it soared.

In town, she kept her head down, told herself she knew the plod of normal. She mastered small talk, let the crows guffaw. Rumours spread. Behind closed doors, she wrapped herself with fledgling surety. Some boys sensed the change and watched her that bit closer. Girls were mean; they called her names.

She learned to carry the changes, practised walking with a wider frame. If she spread her toes apart, she could grip the ground and stay upright. Each season brought another stage of transformation; she wove a nest of gathered twigs and lined it with stray threads and salvaged stems. At night, she dreamed of migration.

Her assailants tracked her to an empty playground. With each strike, she imagined their open palms filled with grain and tucked her wings in close like padding. When they were done, she replayed the attack, added an extra scene where she lifted her neck and pecked out their empty eyes. She didn't report it; she'd learned by now there was no one to defend her but herself. She was not of their kind.

Besides, she was ready now. Where she had been soft and pulpy as an unformed egg, a shell had grown. She pressed her face against the cold train window and let her eyelashes trace the swoop and dive of starlings. In the murmuration, she was alive.

Cut
Andrea Anderson

The lights blink on, fiercely hot and blindingly bright.

Microscope lights.

Operation room lights.

Sterile and jarring and designed to magnify, exaggerate – to judge.

They beat down on your face, melting the thick, caked-on makeup, revealing flushed skin and blurred features. Your palms and hairline are sweaty; the nape of your neck, too, the delicate, jutting swoops of your collarbones. You hope the audience can see it. The glitter of it, the shine.

'Hi,' The Boy says, low and slow, his wide brown eyes fixed on you, intent and calculating, like he's forgotten he's supposed to play nice in the first act. 'I don't think we've met.'

Your heart skips several beats. Heavy, percussive – rhythmic, like war drums. You realize there's no way to communicate this development, this foreshadowing, this vulnerability, to whoever's watching. There's a moth-eaten ball of excitement unraveling in the pit of your stomach, and they don't *know*.

'We have now,' you say with a shy, helpless smile.

Briefly, during intermission, between moments pinched-free and pried-loose backstage, as the director tests you on your lines, reminds you of your marks, tells you what to feel and how to feel and when to feel it – you wonder why you're so tired already.

Didn't the show just start?

Must it really go on?

You're kissed dramatically, possessively, as cymbals crash and raindrops blitz through the theater speakers – you're laid down on a bed of rose petals, on a gingham picnic blanket, surrounded by faded Polaroids and scattered green grapes. You giggle. You beam. Your face hurts. You're given a corsage, and then a Ring Pop, and then an ultimatum.

Eventually, the curtain drops.

Your chest heaves, and your lashes flutter, and The Boy exits stage left; he doesn't look back. Salt-gilded tear tracks swim in the leftovers of your earlier, more innocent blush, and distinctly fingerprint-shaped bruises circle your wrists, your arms – accidents, obviously, because this isn't that kind of story.

You smile and wave, bow and curtsy, accept an oversized bouquet of sweet-smelling flowers from someone with a battered clipboard and a crackling headset.

The applause is thunderous.

The reviews are mixed.

In the Days That Follow
Morgan Quinn

I start spending a lot of time on the internet.

I lie in bed, propped up by my pillow and hers, scrolling through hashtags on Instagram #love #happyfamily #blessed until the dawn chorus splits the silence like a skull against a windscreen, and the feeble sunlight penetrates the voile curtains with contempt. A wholly unsuitable choice for the bedroom, voile, but she'd cocooned herself in them, right there in the middle of the shop, a beseeching image of Verity cast in marble rather than bronze.

I join support groups on Facebook. Swallow other people's stories like comfort. Store them so that I can regurgitate and chew them over at will. Roll them across my tongue and tuck them into the hollow of my cheek until the flavour of their solace fades and I spit them out like a loose molar.

On GoFundMe, I make anonymous donations to a woman whose nose curves slightly to the left in a way that is both familiar and devastating to me.

I retweet petitions to a handful of followers, savouring the indignant punctuation of each demand.

SCRAP 'smart' motorways NOW.

Give PARAMEDICS a pay rise!

STOP the SLAUGHTER of pregnant cows.

I read about the slaughter of pregnant cows. How the foetus is still alive. How it feels pain. Maybe terror. I sign the petition using her name.

YouTube tutorials teach me how to use Photoshop until I can seamlessly splice my face with hers. I drag and drop the baby into her arms. The two of us grin proudly at the camera, teeth bared in perfect rows like Santorini villas.

I WhatsApp the image to her. Stare at the grey ticks until my eyes water, willing them to turn blue.

North by Northwest
Gail Anderson

Your heart remembers: you've been here before. The monument on the right, up high, the rising sun just catching it. Like in that old movie – what was it called? – the one where a man gets chased by a crop duster. This is the place the film ends, isn't it? You walk uphill through tall pines, smelling their sharp, cleansing tang, floor-cleaner fresh. Is the air thinner? There's an acrid smell too, smoke in your hair from early this morning, grubbing around in a cold field at dawn, coaxing a breakfast campfire. Saucepan coffee. Skewered bread, charred and buttered. You'd eaten standing up, felt the warmth of a flame, a surge of confidence. You haven't felt any of this in years. Certainly not since the wedding, definitely not since the divorce. Now the sun is up, the air is hot, and the film's soundtrack blasts in your head. Brass syncopation, trumpets tingle your spine. Your feet beat time, legs aching, a burnt-toast crunch of gravel underfoot. Up ahead, the spark and blink of plate glass, a silver wink through evergreen. You top the path at last – and there it is, in glorious Technicolor. *Rushmore*. Sunlight, the monument café filled with plaid-shirt tourists, the broad jaw of terrace jutting, the sweep of dark valley, the towering up-thrust of granite. A shadow on Washington's face, a rim-lit nose on Jefferson. *Is* this where the film ended? You can't remember. Old clips flash across the screen of your brain. So much deception, control, obsession. You hear sharp words, like teetering on a cliff face. You've been here before, oh yes. And it isn't the final scene, your heart tells you this, but merely a turning point. An old life gone forever, and a woman pulled from a precipice into the arms of a new ending.

Straight On
Fernando Concha

She came in out of the night like a scarecrow by the side of the road. She was wearing a man's coat, and her hair turned white under the lights of my Buick. She didn't ask for help; she wanted a ride and didn't even ask where I was headed to.

Had she asked, I'm not sure what I would've said. The night was long and lonely, and so was the road. I couldn't have sworn the car had been moving for the last hour between one vacant darkness and the next; then I saw her image floating towards me, a dream fragment off of the eye of my steel carcass wanting to swim its way home.

'Care to work up a little conversation, ma'am?'

'I guess it's my job to keep you awake.'

'Only if you don't want us riding in the dark forever.'

'I wouldn't mind that.'

'Keep talking and we may make it to Dawn, AZ."

'I suppose I should tell you that I'm married.'

'That better be your man's coat then.'

'It is. In a way. It's like a keepsake.'

'How's that so?'

'You know how they say, till death do us part?'

'Look, I'm sorry.'

'Oh, don't be. Charles was a wonderful man. Is. I'm not sure to be honest.'

'I know the feeling.'

'But that was ages ago. I'm not over him, that's not what I meant. Wherever he is, he will always be my husband.'

'You must've married young. You still got plenty of time to find yourself a new life.'

'All the time in the world, but this I wouldn't call it living.'

The conversation died alright as it was bound to. So died the engine.

We kept going downhill like baby Moses down the river. Then the lights began to fade, the night closing on us.

It was just the hum of the road for a while, until that gave up as well.

No

Emma J Myatt

It was because you thought nobody liked you. You wanted to impress people.

It was because you were new. Everyone else was happy in their skins and their belonging to this place, and you thought you could do something different, be the first, be the most interesting. It was because he was cool.

It was because once he started, it was gone, so there was no point in stopping. (Might as well lie there until it was finished and keep acting as if you knew what you were doing.)

It was because when he went to the sink, to get the Vaseline, you thought he was going to get you a pillow.

It was because you wanted a boyfriend.

It was because you didn't know how to say no.

It was because you were lonely, sad, unsure of yourself. Because you'd started your periods a few months before and thought you were now a woman, and this was what women did, right?

When the phone calls started, calling you *Whore* and *Slapper*, you told yourself it was because they were jealous.

You told yourself to lie to your parents because you'd get him in trouble, and you saw his eyes when he said that word. Trouble.

After him, it was because there seemed no point in pretending. You said yes, and you told them you loved them. And when they didn't call, you turned to someone else. Because there was always someone else who'd hold you for a few moments. Afterwards.

Years later, you realised it was none of these reasons.

He was wrong, and you'd never been taught what to do. You shouldn't have been at a party like that in the first place. You should not have been drinking.

Years later, when your daughter screams NO at you, you hold her close and wrap her tight and say, Yes. That's what to say if you're ever, ever unhappy with something.

Years later, when your daughter reaches the same age – thirteen and two months – you make sure you always know where she is.

And you make sure she remembers that tiny, enormous word.

The Lover Asks Questions They Cannot Answer
Elaine Mead

Benign questions like *what would you say if I dyed my hair bright green?* They make them laugh, and they don't answer, but they do kiss their cheeks and then their nose and tell them they're funny.

They roll their eyes, wanting more.

What began lightheartedly escalates on tiptoes. A humorous imploring about their reaction should they shave their entire body leads to cymbal crashing sentences about the other's lack of emotional density. They fill the tub with interrogative words, and they thrash in a sea of *what's* and *why's* and *how's*.

The questions gain momentum in the space they leave by not answering them.

What would you do if I jumped off a bridge? What would you do if I lost all my limbs? What would you do if we could time travel? What would you do if you met a future version of me? Who would you pick, my future self or me? What would you do if we got into a fight? Why have we never got into a fight? Why are you so emotionally avoidant? Why don't you love me the way I need?

Why don't you answer me?

One day the questions stop. A false sense of reprieve washes over them before the eggshells start to roar underfoot in the absence of their noise. Then the lover asks a question they haven't heard before.

What would you say if I said I didn't love you anymore?

The question sparks like a firework, unanswerable. Knowing they cannot give the answer the question deserves, the answer that would stem its power, they both watch as the question grows bright as the sun in the hollow of the bedroom ceiling, unrelenting heat beating down on them.

And, like Icarus having flown too close, they begin to burn in a fire of their own making.

After Arlene
Tracy Lee-Newman

I used to have a nightmare that was strangely comforting. It started when I first began to menstruate, and everything that had seemed normal in my mind – the ways I thought and felt – were rendered vague and fishy.

In the nightmare I was in my infant school and sitting in assembly. Then everyone, the children and the teachers and Miss Mulligan who played the old piano, left. But I remained. The lights went off. The Principal, Miss Henderson, came through the double doors from A Block, strode across the parquet floor in front of me, ignoring me. And when the doors to B Block closed behind her, I knew nobody could see or hear me anymore.

I had the dream when all my girlfriends started dating boys. I had it when I went to college, when I screwed up my exams, and when I went to work at Sainsbury's at the fish counter. I had it all through my engagement to Shaun. If more than five nights in a row went by without it, I'd take a double dose of Night Nurse, smoke some weed. That did the trick. When Shaun broke the engagement off, I had the nightmare every night for months. And then I met Arlene.

She said, 'I love your face, your hair, the way you butter-poach a lemon sole.'

She said, 'I have these dreams where everyone I've ever met is chasing me with pickaxes and spades, and in the dream, I know that if they catch me they will bury me alive.'

She held my face. She said, 'So far, I haven't seen you there.'

I didn't love Arlene, and no doubt when I told her that, she saw me in her dream. But I had sex with her. And that night, when the nightmare came and I was back there in that hall alone, I saw myself get up and turn the lights back on and leave.

Pete and Jenny in the Harbour Hotel
Lisette Abrahams

Pete's glad of the job, but oh god, these girls. They might break the hearts of their mothers, but certainly not lovers. There are no lovers, only the men who come and go. Come, and go.

Jenny's the worst of the lot. Cheap and thin in cheap thin vest, her blue-white legs like tense wires stretched taut on top of crap trainers. She saunters past him, eyes flaring 'Fuck you' at him through the foyer.

Before he knew better, he gave her a light. He means *lighter* of course, for he gave her more than the flame. She never returned it – he only had himself to blame when, on his break, he couldn't light his smoke. Next night, she asked for a fiver. She's got a front, earns more than him. It doesn't pay well, working the door in a shitty hotel and watching the girls as the men come and go. He told *her* where to go.

The click, click of his lighter locked behind her door makes him feel sick. He can smell the shit of the powder, water, spoon, and feel the hit that raises red marks on her smoke-grey skin. Pete thinks of his wife, warm, in bed, and doesn't want to picture the men, fists fat with fivers, unfurling those fists and those notes for *this* girl – Jenny, with her bitten nails, hard eyes, foul mouth, thin skin.

This is how Pete thinks of Jenny as he works the door of the Harbour Hotel. And yet, later that night, he, in desperation, will unlock her door, lean over her, and lock his lips to hers. He will press her chest and plead as he breathes, counts, breathes, counts, pleads. *Come back to me, Jenny, come back to me, please.*

They Took the House
Nirvana Dawson

It was hard to drown without water, but we made do.

They cut it off on Thursday. 'Just slowed it down a bit, we have plenty.' You caught the trickle in a glass and held it as tight as your smile while it filled. I wondered which you'd drop first, but your knuckles were whiter than your teeth by now. I focused on them so I didn't have to watch your face fall. You drank that tepid water like we weren't going under.

A paperweight held the bills. Tried to, at least. It teetered on the pile of them, unsteady as we were. The day we got the notice about the power, you picked it up and hurled it through the window. You both broke. A wave of flies and sticky heat poured in. They circled us as we sat right there on the kitchen floor, drinking up the last of the air conditioning, watching the final notices dance across the bench.

'They're taking the house,' you said. You stuck the letter to the fridge, empty and hot. We had tried. We had tried so hard for so long that this letter felt like nothing more than a full stop. We made the demand notices into paper planes and watched them crash. We cried and laughed. We were hungry.

They took the doors first, the windows second. Men in vans arrived at dawn and took the house piece by piece. They untangled the wires and wrapped them around walls like ribbons.

'I didn't think this is what they meant...' Men passed you with the bathtub, and rattling taps shook the rest of your words loose. The sink followed.

It was night by the time they finished, the house loaded into vans brick by brick. They didn't even leave a nail. We stood in the crater, dusty, stunned, watching taillights fade like fireflies.

'They actually took the house.' I found your hand in the darkness. 'They did.' You whispered. We sat together on the cool ground left behind. This piece of earth that used to hold everything. This piece of earth that held us.

Stars yawned above us. We breathed.

On Finding a Body in the Woods
Jo Withers

The dog barks, whines in a way you've never heard, an almost human wail, enough to snap you from your trudging thoughts, he sniffs and pulls and you try to lead him away, knowing things found in woods are never good things and suddenly you see it, pink painted nails in cold grey flesh, and your heart stops, the dog is pacing, knowing something's wrong, wanting to get out of there, and you think about it, think about walking away, but you have a relationship now, the last to see her on earth as her mother was the first, so you breathe and shuffle forwards, but when you see her bare skin and the stretch of her mouth, something unravels inside and she is every woman you've ever known, your sister, your best friend, your future daughter, and you must take her home and bathe her and feed her so she will heal and fly away like a mended bird, but she is dead, so dead, so you take your phone, dial three numbers, say it is an emergency, and they say they will come quickly, but it feels like you're alone with her for days and she seems to rot in front of you, so you stand not looking, looking over and around her, and you don't see the wide white shock of her eyes and you don't see her scratched bare back, and now you'll never be the same, knowing how her body arched in that final moment, how it sits now in soft moss, how green shoots are already sprouting be-tween her thighs so if she was here a little while the roots would con-sume her, and no one, even you, would ever find her, and your own bones will never settle now, you will move house, abandon relation-ships, upend and upturn, because whenever you stop moving you see her reaching fingers, feel roots pulling you under, and when you die, not alone, not in the woods, the last thing you'll see is her face, and in all these years you never knew her but finally her empty mouth is singing in your ear.

Fragments
Jack Barker-Clark

I can tell, the headmaster whispered, unaccustomed to hysteria, *that this was an accident*. The desk was trophy-landscaped – archery, triathlons, squash. *That being said, I will need your account*. W. had gone to the emergency dentists, two pieces of incisor in his fist, a crescent moon punched out of his smile. I had been summoned.

Question: his arms were 'draped over' the metal railings? I nodded. *Making you think of... 'tag team wrestling'?* I nodded. *You proceeded to 'leap off' the concrete?* I nodded. *His head then 'came down' with you?*

I had expected it to rebound gracefully, the taut elastics of a wrestling ring's ropes, but the physics were set, and his teeth had collided with metal. He had sunk down cinematically, and it was all kinds of carnage for the dinner ladies. Orange dust clouds rose up thickly as I scrambled in the dirt, shards of W.'s teeth lost among the hairbands and the wrappers and the gravel.

Afternoon was band practice, K.'s asbestos garage. I played the guitar, the usual embarrassment, three-quarter size, a Ronda, a make nobody had heard of. K.'s grandma made dark Bolognese, wine-drenched, black, was sending us off with it in Tupperware, so many mushrooms, take it, no excuses. I walked home.

Over the fields, stripes of green. It was winter, misty. All the horses had their gilets on. I got in, forked the Bolognese. Usually I washed the dishes, one of my chores – my parents waived it. I shipwrecked in my room, wet pillows, MTV2. The sorrowful glances my mum flung me whenever she climbed the stairs to check on me made me want to die.

In the corridors the next day, I looked halcyon, but my guilt was drowning me in my own throat. Colliding noises startled me, the bell a rosy clatter of glass. W. was here, smiling, upright, the successful specimen of his own emergency dentistry. He looked as normal, shrugged. I never asked him whether they'd replaced the whole of both incisors or glued back on the dust-glazed fragments. We raided the tuck shop. We traded our Pokémon. It never came up.

Amber
Michael Salander

A man unfurls his fingers and finds within his palm a faded photograph of an unknown city sleeping beneath a silent moon. Closing his hand, he feels the moon and the city crumbling to dust. He watches it falling slowly through his fingers to the pavement, like a powder of amber fluttering from the wings of a moth in the cold night air. And he thinks: I am a man who does not belong here. I am a man who leaves an imprint on the darkness, to be filled by loss and solitude when I am no longer here.

Later, in a clinical white room that smells of sweat, a security guard watches CCTV footage of a man in a street, a man who appears to be just standing there doing nothing, but who then seems to simply disappear; not in the sense that he walks away and beyond the reach of the camera, but that, impossibly, he slowly vanishes. The guard keeps replaying the scene and becomes obsessed with running the clip backwards.

In reverse, some kind of vapour or smoke, perhaps, seems to rise upwards from the pavement and into the man's hand, which closes around it, but it's too indistinct and grainy to be certain of anything.

Walking home later, the guard feels a disturbing sense of unease. He is disorientated, as though he could easily become lost in the familiarity of his hometown. He feels drawn to the street with the CCTV camera, to the spot where the man must have been standing.

Arriving at what he believes must be the exact location, he finds himself standing outside the window of a charity shop, its display of donations illuminated by an amber streetlight. He notices a box of old black and white photographs, and a large moth is frantically fluttering against the window in its attempts to reach the streetlight beyond.

The next day, in a clinical white room that smells of sweat, a security guard watches some CCTV footage of a man in a street, a man who appears to be just standing there doing nothing but who then seems to simply disappear.

Withered Flowers
Jake W Cullen

I'll get there eventually, I'll just close my curtains and tap away. Tap away until it's as pristine and as perfect as it can be. Atmosphere set, I've my pot of Anji Bai Cha (that's a kind of tea), incense burning, a desk of small potted plants (just watered), *Howl, Kaddish & Other Poems* on the desk (bookmark resting where 'Sunflower Sutra' begins) and mellow lo-fi hip-hop playing quietly. I knew it, with this kind of prep, I couldn't fail.

Molten heat stoked the forest fires not far from here. By midday, abundant clouds congregated like politicians voting to take money away from the poor and razorblade rain cut at my thick windows. Smoke plumed as the flames were temporarily extinguished.

I reached under my desk and flicked on the air purifier. I sipped at the warm tea, the bitter taste and the sweet smoke from the incense met near my nose and exchanged compliments. I read the opening line of that Ginsberg poem. *You were never no locomotive, Sunflower, you were a sunflower!* The gentle bass of the hip-hop kissed my ears. I typed a few lines of my own, and I knew *I* could do it.

The hail hurled in sideways, smashing windows, denting rusty cars and knocking the heads off of withered flowers. Winds sent the immense piles of trash flying, and the homeless sheltered in bus stations.

I watched the lavender smoke swirl from the incense sticks and dance with the curled tips of my desk plants. I watched darkness escape the leaves as I squeezed the tea strainer, it swam and flourished like piranha in a fish tank. A car alarm sounded from the outside, and I felt my perfect writing atmosphere diminish. I turned up the calming hip-hop.

Cold and hot air clashed and shot bolts of electricity at the smoking forests, black birds shot from what was left of the branches. Wind sent the smoke hurling through alleyways, streets, homes and bus stations.

I got up and pulled open the curtains. I look outside and think about opening the window, just the once. A red-light blinks under my desk.

Made
Fiona Lynch

It doesn't matter if the edges are a little raggedy. Take whatever you have decided to work with – paper, cardboard, fabric – and cut out two small pieces that match (near enough). Circles, squares, rectangles, it's up to you. Bring the two pieces together, and carefully glue or stitch until only a small opening remains. (If you are stitching, please don't use a machine, it's important to take time to do this by hand. And don't be fussing over blanket stitch or back stitch, just something that will keep things in, nice and tight).

Find something that is about you, just you, and place it inside the little pocket you have made. Perhaps a lock of hair, a photo, a line from a letter you wrote. Maybe a petal from a plant you nurtured, or holiday findings – pretty shells, upturned stones. Finish sealing the bag and bless it with a kiss when done. Tuck it in the casing under your pillow, or burrow in a bedside drawer.

On the nights you feel unmoored, reach for your pocket and hold it decisively to your heart. Close your eyes, breathe and repeat three times:

I am here.
I am everything I have ever made.
I am everything I have ever touched, by hand and heart.
I am as simple as a smile, as complex as a corner.
I am here.

Run a finger over coarse edges, and feel for names and places. Caress uneven joins and pay attention to the weight of your little bag. Remind yourself the difference between flotsam and jetsam is intent, and questions are nearly always looking to mate with answers. Breathe as if breath is a precious borrowing, and contemplate the wealth of a pulse in your tiny purse.

Made for Each Other
Jason Jackson

Sometimes she thinks they've been together too long, but then he comes home with guitar strings, and she lets him wrap them like jewellery around her ankles, her wrists. One day he spends hours tinkering with the clock until the second hand plays a biological rhythm – *du-dum, du-dum* – in perfect time with her heart. She loves him best when he lets his fingernails grow; she takes her curved silver scissors, holds his hand gently – *snip! snip! snip!* – before blowing on each fingertip, a craftswoman at work.

They have yellow shirts and sixteenth-century art; horror films and ice sculpture; tomatoes; the poetry of John Keats.

One day, she wakes in an otherwise-empty bed, a creased white sheet where his body should be and a hollow in the pillow for his head. Outside, there is a smudged, smeary sky.

In the garden, she rips daffodils from the soil, throws snails at the wall, crushes them underfoot.

In the kitchen, she makes tiny piles of sugar, salt, pasta and rice on the cold linoleum.

In the bathroom, everything fills with water, everything overflows.

She climbs barefoot into the attic, splinters in her toes from the rough wooden beams. The air is suffocating, and there are spiders in the corners, swift shadows of rats. She wants to stay, drinking drips from the water tank, licking dust from the eaves. She'll strip naked, her skin will sag on her bones, her callouses will harden, and her eyes will become blind; she'll be a tiny translucent mole-creature, or some strange fish from the depths where the sun can't reach.

And then: his key in the door; his quick, calm step; his *hello there, hello, hello.*

And the rush of it: love, like the bitterest of lemons, and taking the stairs two at a time. The *jumping-into-arms* of it, the kisses and the tears. The *never-leave-me-never-leave-me-never-leave-me-alone* of it.

The *knowing-what-home-means:* the hurt and the hunger of *never-let-me-go.*

Sticky Hands

Jen Knox

My fingers, like pale birch, stayed cold in the winter. I learned to ball my hands in fists or snuggle them in pockets, which made me somehow smaller. Unimaginable. But smallness had its advantages. I could hide. I could peel the icing off the raisin bread my father kept on the counter, for instance, using the delicacy of my index finger and thumb.

My sister's fingers extended beyond my own, despite my seniority on this planet. She was two and a half years younger and full of the sovereignty a child with stature often has. We pressed our palms hard, and I longed for her strength. I asked her to open the black raspberry jam. She asked me to reach around the couch cushions when she lost the remote.

'Look at her hands,' a girl said. My fingers were contracted like my body always was in my twenties, but this was the first time anyone pointed it out. We were at a party. I was supposed to be laughing or dancing, but the visibility of trauma begs itself known. I didn't understand that then, nor did I understand how to relax and let go.

Young years, I drank. Until an old nail that had seen too much caught the pad of my hand, just below my index finger. The skin tore, and the sheer amount of blood hypnotized me. I was too stunned to be embarrassed, so I sat and waited for what was next. Waiting for what was next was my modus operandi then. At the bar, I wrapped a cloth napkin around my hand and tuned in, listened to the throbbing.

It took years to slow down long enough to feel the bark of a tree, the texture of stone, the flow of water and the warmth of my husband's cheek. I push down into the earth and spread my fingers wide, unapologetically, as I push my body up mornings. Days, the rhythm of life pulses with each keystroke. Each mudra. Each opportunity to accept and release. My hands have learned to reach out, offer support. Accept. Receive.

Ways to Vanish
Emily Roth

There'd been a noise in the old lady's house. A crack. A boom. *Something popped*, someone told us.

We rode our bikes down the dirt path to investigate. Except you, Jess, because we couldn't find you.

You'd taken the commuter train to the city with your babysitting money. We wouldn't know this until the next day at lunch. *That's allowed?* we'd ask, incredulous. You'd smile over your Diet Coke.

The old lady's house looked the same as always. Rotting clapboard, straggling pansies along the walk, upper window flickering.

We waited, expecting you to roll up on your Schwinn beach cruiser. We didn't know at that very moment you were emerging from the subway, that the pavement glistened from a storm just ended.

The seconds stretched before we felt the first raindrops. We went quiet, listening, the mystery softly rippling before us.

I breathed in, smelling musk and campfire. *Old lady smell*, we decided.

~

The old lady burst. The news would break at lunch the next day. *They found her feet and a pile of ash. No blood, no guts. Just smoke.*

I'd study the curve of your lips as you listened.

Later, we'd return to the house, all of us this time.

I'd consider telling you what you missed the night before: the acrid smell, the rain, the dying light. But instead I'd ask what you saw in the city.

Nothing, really, you'd say. *I just wanted to disappear for a bit.*

Biking home, I'd wonder, can love burn you from the inside out?

~

As time would barrel forward – at twenty, fifty, eighty – each time I'd drive past the old lady's house, even long after its demolition, I'd imagine your forehead pressed to the train window, watching the city shrink behind you.

I would forget our friends, someday. I would forget your face, but I wouldn't forget your name. Jess, like a crack of thunder in my skull. Jess, like a siren. Jess, like church bells. In my last moments, I'd part my lips around the syllable, but my children, hovering around my bed, would mistake the sound for a death rattle.

Borderline
Birgit Wildt

'Please keep to the allocated time slots!'

I was used to resistance, but this format was new. The gallery, once made for us, now haunted us with conduct signs and behaviour symbols. Observing and being observed in a space for cultural relations seemed like an affront.

'Please keep within the markings!'

We should step back or step aside or on the spot, and mind our distance. The gallery, once a flexible space, was marked with way-finding arrows and two-metre indicators.

'Please make use of the hand sanitiser!'

We were safely led to a Warhol. You in front of me. I hardly followed the announcements but your scent, a touch of Gaultier, *Scandal*, I thought, suited Andy. I tried to see what you were seeing, just to make sure that the world we share is still the one we both knew. We live in a networked society, a negotiated environment. *#MeToo* wasn't me, and I hardly communicate in public, persistently wary of the responses of others. The gallery brought us together to debate and critique, but critique isn't fixed or paralysed but free to roam. Free was the impulse pushing me as I spoke impatiently, in fragments, busily protecting my image. Safeguarded by the order of this regulated exhibition, I kept in line with the progression until, eventually, I stood at the front of the queue. Embodied features attracted my gaze. Marilyn, I wheezed and grabbed a chair.

'Please don't move objects!'

I didn't move objects, only a chair from the side, but, of course, a chair is an object. I missed the sign hidden away as I hid my resistance, which was not an active resistance but a personal struggle with upcycled gallery etiquettes. This new language of authority didn't fit, and I followed your scent on the way out...

The Beach at Dugort
Chris Lee

Welcome to the scatterings. First there was Danny Mahon. Climbed Slievemore on a rain-sodden night. A bottle of Paddy inside him and no heed to warnings. Reached the top, sang his favourite song, 'No Surprises' by Radiohead, then plunged over the sheer cliff that tumbled him down to Dugort strand. This we speculate, of course; we weren't there. It was only Danny himself, flamed up with the malt, raging like a banshee, spitting his soul out into the angry air of Achill Island.

Look behind you, that's Slievemore, craggy and spiteful in the whip of the wind betimes, but now as meek as an April lamb, sleeping in a meadow. You can't be taking the weather in Achill for granted. Barley sweet sunlight one minute and the Devil's own downpour the next.

We don't bury folk on Achill; we charr them to cinders, then sprinkle the ashes here, where the wild Atlantic is tamed by the crook of Belmullet's arm. We let them float away into the lapping water and rise occasionally on a gust of spindrift. Returned to the mist, they will have their vengeance only in soft rain.

Then there was Bridgit Latouche. She married a Frenchman and repented at leisure. I found her hanging by the damn at Lough Acorrymore. She'd been on her own for three years, but the torch I carried never lit me bravely to her door. There you go, Bridgit, spare a ghost's blessing for a cowardly heart.

My name is Barry Kennedy, a second cousin much removed from the famous Americans. I drowned here at Dugort when the great squall of last February battered me against the pier. I'd just tethered the fishing boat and lost my footing on the granite. I washed up round Keel way three days later. My friend Conor McCarthy found me. He was out walking the beach in a scarlet dress the way he liked to.

They'll be burning us all before the decade's out, the last few denizens born here. Maybe the currents will mix us together in Blacksod Bay, and our dreams will slowly settle like sand. I'd like that.

The Prettiest Star
Lee Hamblin

It may well be the coldest winter on record, but when the power cuts again, I go sit outside and look up at the black and white sky. In moments unpolluted, it breathes a thousand twinkles; twinkles that may already have died, which I suppose means that some of what I'm seeing are ghosts... and I wonder, is there more illumination in death than life?

High above, and surrounded by admirers, the prettiest star shines even brighter: she is a stunning 1960's pearl-eared Hollywood starlet, frozen mid waltz on the red carpet. She has a white fur draped across her wrist, probably mink, flashlight-melting sunglasses over her eyes, probably Chanel, and, for the life of me, I can't remember her name, and I so wish I remembered only the beautiful things in this world.

Across the street, elongated shadows sculpted by candlelight skulk about. Curtains snatch open as tempers blister. On the second floor, the bent old man appears on the balcony frenzy-sucking a cigarette. On each plumy exhale, he turns and yells into the room behind him. There is no one to listen, his family gone now. He is the ghost of the leader of men he once was, his family, just ghosts.

You hear before you see. Over by the docks tonight, same as last Saturday. Ash falls as the bent old man screams at the blood-reddening sky. I call over to him, not that I have words of comfort, just so he's not alone, *Hey, Captain,* I say. He quiets and disappears into the dark, and it seems I've forgotten how to cry.

I tell myself that memories live in our hearts, and hearts are made of love, and a song begins playing in my head. It's a song from a time when I loved and was loved, a moment when everything in this world truly was beautiful, and even this hellfire on earth won't make me forget.

Patterns
Rick White

On the rainiest days of August's turbid swan song, we take to the kitchen floor. Swirling loops of poster paint with childish fervour onto torn paper, later displayed with pride on the refrigerator door. Like every parent ever, I will say that although we were only playing, you really can make out the glint of infant talent, a natural flair, an eye.

You say – *don't do it that way, Daddy*, when I try to apply the same abstractionist method to the macaroni pictures your teacher sets as homework. You want the little bronze shapes within the lines of PVA glue, equidistant, just so. You sprinkle glitter looking over your shoulder like a timid seamstress in some Victorian novel, expecting a rebuke. I wonder who taught you to paint with fear.

I will begin to notice the order in which you put your dolls away, always in exactly the same place. Dead-eyed nineties it-girls shooting me scorn when I walk past your open door and hear you talking.

You will choose maths and physics over art. Notating the very fabric of the Universe itself – distilling the infinite to try and reach an answer you will never find, but when I tell you that hell, even though I don't believe in God, perhaps there is a plan for all of us you will say – *where is the proof?*

You will keep careful track of every twenty-eight days, placing your faith in the deathless lunar cycle, cursing every waxing and waning without a stellar collision from which new planets may be formed.

You will find yourself alone on the first Wednesday of every month. You won't realise why until you check his calendar, credit card receipts, phone bill. Numbers cannot lie.

You will visit me every Friday, and although you'll try and try, there is no way to determine when I will be lucid. But on clear, cold evenings, we will sit outside for a while. You and I tessellated together under a crocheted blanket – so small, so transient – beneath the constellations, the night has somehow stitched together for a moment, just for us.

She Understands the World Through What It Is Not
Donna L Greenwood

The apple is not green. She drops it into the brown bag which is not plastic and will not choke the seas. She nods to the stallholder who is not a threat. She pays for the apples and walks through the yawning ginnels of the market.

She absorbs the scents and sights that do not remind her of home. The prickly woollen cardigans hanging on strings are not the turquoise swirls and sequined flashes of the markets of her childhood. The baying of the traders is not the birdsong chatter of the bazaars she remembers. She does not buy golgappa for the journey home.

She passes a crowd of boys who snarl at her and shout words she does not understand. She doesn't look at them as she quickens her pace.

A man who is not the same as her stands in front of her and looks down with concerned, not-brown eyes. 'Are you okay?' he asks. She shakes her head at the man and runs away, pulling her scarf over her bruises as she goes.

She reaches the house. The man who stands in the doorway waiting for her is not love. He is not the large yellow sun; he is a small, white winter. He opens the jaws of his arms and swallows her up. He is not gentle. He is not warm. He is not her mother singing 'Moon Uncle'. He is not children playing in rainbow puddles in dusty streets. As he locks the door behind her, she understands what he is and what he never was.

Art Project: Woman Freed
Karen Jones
SUMMER 2021 FIRST PLACE

He'd been turning her into art for two years. At first changing the way she dressed, from suits to hippy-chic, her hair from tight ponytail to rambling, dancing, screaming curls, her make-up from mask to nude, her jewellery from a single, slender chain to beads and teeth and feathers. He took a blowtorch to her stilettos and let her watch their power melt. Together they twisted the remains into a mishmash of nothing more than painful memories and mounted them as a sculpture in the middle of the daisy-strewn front lawn. They titled the piece 'Volcano'. Bare-soled and bare-souled, she became truly his.

Her mind was more difficult to mould. Dagger sharp, her cynicism cut him. Whale song made her feel 'a bit stabby', she said. Pan pipes made her dry heave. One more set of wind chimes, and she'd show him how effective they could be as a noose. It was the sky that won her over. She'd never seen a meteor shower nor a shooting star – always too busy or too tired, no matter how many times over the years he'd tried to entice her into the garden. The night they lay on a blanket next to 'Volcano' while the universe put on a cosmic ballet, she cried. He wanted to hold her, but she pushed him away. 'This is just for me,' she told him. He nodded, though reached for her hand, and she gripped him as though she was sinking, falling through space.

Months on, he continued to work on her. They had agreed there'd be no funeral. She was his before the illness took her; she would be his ever after. He polished and arranged her bones in a way he considered a better fit for her final self – looser. Her hair shorn, scattered, but glued in random, pleasing place. Her teeth crushed, pressed into a shale-like smile. And a single foil star, where her heart used to beat.

.

62

Raised Curtain
Simon Linter
SUMMER 2021 SECOND PLACE

Imagine everyone in the nude. That's what they thought when they stood before the closed blue curtain. The theatre's atmosphere was stale, what with the odd throaty cough and phlegmy sneeze that sounded. They were certain they heard a baby crying and a smartphone's ringtone; that annoying ringtone old Nokia mobiles used to have. They asked themselves why would anyone choose that and why were any smartphones' sound on, especially when they were only minutes away from their entrance. If only the audience could be quiet; if only they could be patient; if only they could be accepting; if only they could love. They hated each and every one of the audience because they knew them intimately. So-called family and so-called friends had gathered for this occasion because they would see their faces on television, in the background, in the front row, on repeat after repeat after repeat on cable. *Look, there I am*, some would say. They wanted to imagine everyone in the nude because that's what the expression said to do at times like this. Calms the nerves... But so does vodka.

A cough.

A sneeze.

An SMS.

A familiar voice whispered a comment about how his entrance would transpire.

His?

Maybe they were talking about something or someone else. It didn't matter because they'd have their revenge in a matter of seconds because a drum roll had started, a fanfare played, and the curtains opened to gasps. They were dressed in a tight-fitting blue dress made up of sequins and fake jewels; stilettos with heels that could double as weapons; and a diamond tiara that reflected camera flashes.

Their father huffed, shook his head and stomped out of the theatre, leaving the mother with no option but to become a curling wife. Their siblings remained rooted to their seats in shock, unable to applaud, and none of them could see where the incisions had been made, or had noticed the long hormoned metamorphosis, or could hardly recognise their own – they had to carefully choose their defining pronoun.

You'll see your faces on television, she thought and smiled.

Since the Shipyard Closed
Katja Sass
SUMMER 2021 THIRD PLACE

Since the shipyard closed down, we're all just half-formed: us kids, whose childhoods have been faded out like an 80s record; the shells of our burnt-out buildings and our burnt-out parents; the boat skeletons that never got their flesh.

Last Thursday we were all down at the dock, sharing a joint, when three of us saw Jenson get up. I looked away when he stepped off. I thought *what's the point of watching him? I don't want to learn how to do it.*

Susie kept her eyes on him the whole time. Her dad was the first to go into the water that winter. She used to come down to plead with people not to do the same, but I think she actually only goes there now to watch, and she really does watch: she counts out loud as they take one step, two, three, a shaky fourth, and she holds her breath for the last few seconds – sometimes even a minute – until they collapse away from sight, like a punctured buoy.

Susie and Lola, my oldest friends, are fleshy bits that hang off the skeleton of this town. While they dangle, they smoke, drink, have sex too young with grey-faced men who haven't jumped yet. Their moms don't know where to find them between supper and dawn.

I went with them once to the empty Catholic school on the hill. They smashed the stained-glass windows and sprayed dicks on the old desks. Lola said *there's no God in town anymore*, before she pissed into the Virgin Mary water feature.

I go there now sometimes, to the chapel, to sit in one of the dusty pews, imagine God is still here, just discarded like the rest of us.

At first, I prayed the water would rise up and sweep us all off the docks, save us the pain of choosing; once, last spring, I walked to the edge and pleaded, but it didn't come and get me.

So now I pray for Jenson and the others. I pray that, under the dock, there's actually light, music playing, and angels who take turns to swim up and collect the souls.

Almost Everything I Know About Lemons
I Learned from My Mother
Morgan Quinn
SUMMER 2021 FOURTH PLACE

I know they are essential for staying willowy thin, squeezed into luke-warm water each morning and swallowed in dainty sips at the breakfast bar. I know to tell my teachers, when they ask, that I had cornflakes, or porridge, or toast. Lemons can also be used in cakes. Their buttercup rind grated and mixed with glittering crystals of sugar, slick cubes of butter, powdery puffs of flour. I don't learn this from my mother. These are not her lemons.

Not all lemons are small. The world's largest lemon was almost twelve pounds in weight. My mother tells me this as she nibbles on wisps of menthol smoke and casts her eyes over my honeydew stomach, my spaghetti squash thighs.

A lemon is actually a misunderstood berry. They don't fit in with the sweet, plump strawberries, fickle and changeable as the moon. They are unanimously shunned by blueberries, affluent and pretentious. They are too afraid to approach the tart, sharp-tongued raspberry. Lemons are the loneliest of fruits.

I know how lemons can stop unwanted things from growing. My mother teaches me this as we sit on the bathroom floor. Her squeezing the acidic juice into a bowl before slowly picking out the pips and placing them in a slick pile on the linoleum. Me clutching the torn strap to my shoulder and thinking about how vegetables don't belong in the fruit bowl. She places her hand on my face, sugary sweet. Tells me this always works. This almost always works. Leaves me alone with the juice and the pips and the echo of her lingering gaze prickling across my skin.

I know that lemons are guaranteed to leave a sour taste in your mouth.

Strawberry Nocturne
Courtney Harler

Three hours past midnight, and she's in the kitchen eating fresh strawberries straight from a bowl in the fridge. She stands in the open door's light, pink bathrobe cinched tight just above her hips. The strawberries are rinsed, but she tastes the grit of their skins, the seeds popping between her molars. She eats down to the white tops and green leaves, then tosses the strawberry heads into the sink.

She remembers how all the strawberries in England came from Egypt. She remembers the one child missing during their years overseas. She remembers how his birthday is soon, a day in the early spring. Last year she learned that all the swallows return to San Juan Capistrano each year on his day. Every year, same day. The same day she's marked for almost seventeen years. She wants to go there but can't make the trip this year. Next year, she promises herself. And every year thereafter. It's a miracle, they say. An annual miracle.

Her son at what would've been five years old joins her in the kitchen tonight. He comes to her, at different ages, saying what little boys might say. Tonight, he's just past toddlerhood; his face is starting to lose that pudgy baby roundness. He wants night strawberries too, but wants them cut into halves, straight through the green stems. He wants to dip them in vanilla yogurt, drizzled with honey and sprinkled with chopped pecans. She's happy to oblige, pleased by his adult palate, one she's cultivated since conception with her own body. She fed him fruits and nuts via her womb, and all the dark, iron-rich spinach leaves. After birth, he sampled the juices of carrots and beets through her breastmilk. At one year old, he chewed strawberries for the first time and promptly broke out into a rash all over his bottom.

He's been waiting these four years for more strawberries, and she waits now, watching for signs of a dangerous allergic reaction. All is well; he swallows each bite. She hears the migratory birds winging their way from Goya, Argentina, which may as well be England, may as well be Egypt.

Bug Facts
Timothy Boudreau

Tomorrow you'll look up how caterpillars pee and what kind of spiders are big enough to eat birds and why a dragonfly would want to fly backward.

It's sleepover weekend. The five-year-old can't know how much pain you or your wife are in, the thick ribbon of scar under the partially peeled layer of your surgical glue, the hip your wife tweaked, or is it arthritis; the doctors can't decide.

When you go upstairs, you'll be sleeping alone, but it's fine; it's just the arrangement. She sets up the spare bedroom, joins your grandson there. She likes it better. It gives you some space; at least one of you may get a decent night's sleep.

She'll sleep with her body curled toward her grandson, the ceiling fan blowing the silver-blond of her bangs. She won't sleep until he does, which won't happen till he talks himself out, tall tales and sleepy ones, tales from the big book on the shelf beside the bed, the spiders, honeybees and dragonflies filling his head as he lies back, facing the ceiling, eyelids fluttering shut.

Upstairs you'll sleep the untroubled sleep of the sufficiently drugged. You'll be first up in the morning, and after you make breakfast and cuddle your grandson on the couch, you'll Google his insect questions from the night before. When your wife rouses herself from the spare bedroom, your grandson will run bright-eyed to her with his newest bug facts.

You and the five-year-old will carry the conversation. Your wife will sip her coffee and watch the boy, beam at him, in fact. She will not make eye contact with you.

Caterpillars don't pee, but they poop all the time, black blotches on perfectly green leaves. A giant South American spider eats hummingbirds, lizards, and rodents, injects them with poison before drinking their insides, leaves the husks of the corpses behind. Some dragonflies prefer to fly backwards to visit the places they've already been. Maybe they think there are happier times back then, something magical before everything started to go wrong.

One Every Four Days
Naoise Gale

I think I was on the train when you slit your wrists. Listening to Radiohead, musing melancholy, oblivious to the rivulets of blood, the last-minute doubts, the deleted texts. I had seen you the day before, a smiling pixelated face. We were going to dance the Time Warp. I don't know if I loved you, but you made me feel human. Sexy thing, all legs. Nineteen. Dynamite.

They resurrected your ghost on Halloween, no kidding. Devils laughed and vomited into buckets. So many bones, very little flesh. I like to think of you wearing your Belstaff, quietly dead and meringue stiff, white and unbloodied. Who am I kidding? Your final violence ploughed into my stomach and left me mangled origami. Some wretched parade of grief. Unjustified, I felt, a mute drifting friend, no messages between us. Too distant for that last honour roll – you named who mattered and who didn't. On that night, I sent my mother back to England and binged to remind myself I was alive. Even the pointless stars were daggers. The toilet glared in their pharmaceutical light.

After the snot and the ferrous rage, after so many gluttonous, jerking afternoons, I stopped feeling your loss. I watched documentaries on suicide dry-eyed. I forgot the myriad damage and tied a half-hearted noose around my own neck, called it contagious. The family hated us for unknown reasons, and Russel Group uni tossed your name into a scrapheap of other lost, delusional souls. Worked too hard, didn't work hard enough, insufficient even in death. They erased the word suicide and murmured *very sad, what a waste*. Rang at-risk students, two-minute phone call, then silence.

We sang vigils for you in cluttered bedrooms. Unlearned tears and grew babies in undisturbed wombs. Forgot how to love you. None of us thought of waste, or potential, or future. You were here, and then you were gone. You blazed, and we didn't care if you made it or not. Rather a third than a corpse. Rather a drop-out than a corpse. The anorexic withered and pressed pictures of you. We loved you.

We loved you.

Rabbit Lane
Julie Evans

Rabbit Lane is where you go when your dad says why don't you try a bloody smile for once, or when your sister's taken your stuff but doesn't get told off because she's 'only little'. It's where you go when your mum says that your hair is like rats' tails, and why can't you go to Mario's and have a nice, neat bob cut like Alice Whittaker's.

It's a climb up Rabbit Lane. It's not really a lane; it's a path across the moor. By the time you get to the top, you might feel better if it's sunny. But you might feel worse if it's raining or a howling wind, because there's no cover on the moor until you get to the Druid Stone.

On Rabbit Lane, you can feel the sky squeezing you, like the way your boot presses water out of the moss. You can see for miles. You can see the pylon chain like a giant's bracelet across the hillsides as far as the reservoir; you can see the village, curled like a cat at the bottom of the valley. It's like you're heavy, but you're also on top of the world.

On Rabbit Lane, there's a place where someone keeps a porn mag under a big stone. The pages are damp and stick together, and you know some perv's been jacking off with it, so best rub your fingers on the grass if you look. Not that it's much of a turn-on: everything is just pink and fleshy, like tonsils.

If you're lucky, you might see some foxes or a roe deer. And sometimes rabbits pop up, the rabbits of Rabbit Lane. In sunlight, the red veins glow inside their ears.

Sit down beside the Druid Stone. You can lean against it and watch the snipes wheeling and whirring overhead. Lick it, see if its magic will make that embarrassing patch of eczema behind your knee disappear.

Then wait there long enough for them to start worrying about the time and thinking about that weirdo with the quad bike. Then they'll be nicer to you when you get home.

The Price You Pay
Kristen Loesch

I work at the alleyway that changes you into somebody else, if you go all the way through.

It belongs to my grandparents. When Nana first let me run the front desk, she said, the customers have to bloody *pay*, mind. We ain't runnin' a charity. If they wanna change for cheap, there's an off-license round the corner, eh? And I said, Nana, your voice sounds funny to me. Are you putting on a terrible cockney accent? And she said, oh, bollocks, makes sense though, don't it, because I went one yard down me alleyway this morning, grabbed some stray shoes, always findin' shoes ain't I! Bloody socks-only policy, that's your grand-dad's idea that were—

Was, Nana, I said, but it was hopeless.

Our customer base is diverse, but the majority want to be rich, famous, good-looking, talented. We regularly churn out monarchs, shipping magnates, and the people in Cirque du Soleil who can hurtle themselves through tiny upright hula hoops. But a few show up here because there's something they can't leave behind. I listen as they cry, as they describe their life stories, all the grief, hope, battles, boredom, stress, small children, sick children. And I tell them, listen, our alleyway can give you exactly what you want, that's why my grandfather built it – but if you go all the way, you're going to lose the life story.

I always have to lower my voice in case Nana stops singing along to Oliver Twist in the background.

Sometimes they go through anyway, and when they come out the other end, young, flowy, happy, fake, I promise to follow them on Instagram.

Others choose to go home. Cor-blimey, Nana will say, when I tell her. Reckon they must really like the shoes they're walkin' in.

Ready for the Words
Vanessa Couchman

That's where you lived, the crumbling cottage with wet patches on the walls and rotting thatch riddled with holes. An ash sapling pokes up through a crack. The windows are dark, sightless eyes. No one dares go there now.

In your time, the panes shone with firelight in the winter's dusk, scribbles of woodsmoke curled up towards the sky, and the scent of herbs and fruits bubbling in the pot crept around the door.

They said Mother Jones was beyond help, but you laid your hands on her belly and whispered your secret words. She was soon up out of her bed again, waving her stick at us children for stealing the apples and chasing the hens.

When Tom Bailey fell off the hayrick, the bone stuck out of his elbow like the wishbone from the Sunday chicken. He screamed fit to wake the sleepers in the churchyard. You spread your fingers over his arm, and his red heat poured into them. We watched with eyes big as marbles as the bone shrank back under the flesh and the skin closed over it. Not a mark or a scar.

Tom went around showing his miracle elbow to everyone. You could do magic, he said. You got a few eggs for your pains.

And you helped Mrs Brooks avoid a tenth mouth to feed, although people only talked about that in furtive whispers. She wasn't the only one who slipped hooded across your threshold at dusk.

You said you'd tell me the words on a Christmas Eve while the church bell rang. When I was ready and old enough.

But when they dragged you onto the cart that sparkling frosty morning, no one spoke for you. I ran and hid in the woods, my apron over my head. And when they put you on trial in the town, no one defended you. And when they tied you to the stake in the market square, no one gave you comfort. You cursed us while the flames rose, we heard.

And when the plague came, I had none of your words to heal it. I never grew old enough.

We Were Together Once
Salena Casha

I first noticed the car in the July of lockdown on an early run when I could be bothered for an early run. Blue tarp crinkled and hooked under half-exposed sedan doors, parallel parked by a meter between a black Lexus and an empty space.

Plastic flowers, dewed azaleas and daisies, poked out from under the hood.

It was the same summer I started showering twice and then three times a day when I'd had a beer or two.

I looked for the car whenever I left the house. Spotty appearances during the week but Sundays, like Church. Once, I saw a woman in a sunhat peeling the tarp back. Less than five feet tall wearing Birkenstocks and a tan cardigan. I forced myself into a jog and didn't look back as I passed, but I thought about her the whole way home.

Sometimes, when I was at the sink, I'd crack my back for my older self. Posturize. Flex my fingers in the suds and imagine how she slept, if she leaned the seat all the way back or tried to lie down in the back, curled. If anyone ever tapped on the windows. If she was alone.

If she had someone.

The water always left my skin bright red for a half-hour after, clean. Vessels opening. It was the summer that I stopped running into pieces of him by surprise and sat with it instead on purpose, put the scenes under a microscopic eye. Dissected the sweat left by my bra, a hand resting on a knee. Autumn leaves crunching under tires. The coffee on the bedside table. The slamming front door.

Shirt licking my body from a late-night run, May, I saw the car parked under a streetlamp, a mile from home. The passenger side opened; two sandalled feet set on the ground. A man's voice rose into the asphalt night. Too far to hear, but the sound keened in my chest, my stomach. I watched the feet, toes pointed away from the car as if to stand.

We stood there for minutes together and no one moved and the next morning, she was gone.

Hiraeth

Kathy Hoyle

Nanna is cockles dipped in vinegar, lardy bread, sugared tea, warm stottie cakes, cold feet on stone hearth. Nets whitened in the bucket on Sundays, same bucket we piss in through winter to avoid the outhouse. Peg dollies in flowered scraps, skipping rope counts in the back yard, *and a one and a two*, pinny pocket with a cotton hanky for bairn's tears.

Grandad is black and white cowboy films, cold arse on stone seawall, waiting outside with crisps and pop, smoking rollies, thick foamed pints, *Shhh, don't tell Nanna we popped in*. Thruppenny mixups, *bring the change!* Bellowing at the horses, unluckiest bugger alive. Polished gramophone, crackled music, and a one and a two, small feet balanced on wool slippers, *this one's called the foxtrot.*

Mam is blue eyeshadow and slingbacks; Dad is donkey jacket and muck. Waving, on Friday nights, from the good room window, car taillights blinking in the dusk. Bristled kisses and perfume, lingering. Sister is dark curls, tossed in the wind, kicking burnt orange leaves with shiny new school shoes, matching woollen hats, trying to keep up, *wait for me, Kidda!* Crabbing on mossed rocks, wet socks and wellies on the back step, *keep that step clean, it's just been scrubbed!*

Home is shrieking gulls, amble cobles, masts clanking in the harbour, buggying down slag heaps, the biting north-east wind, *rub your hands together like this*. Milksnow skies, furious crashing sea, sand dune picnics, Sunday night baths, drinking hot chocolate, watching the coal fire dance while Mam brushes out the knots.

Fear is 'Maggie Thatcher, milk snatcher', Dad's face, pale and worn, Mam selling her best rings, counting out ha'pennies on the kitchen table, *and a one and a two*, pit wheel halting, bellies rumbling, hearts breaking... lives crumbling.

Boiled Eggs
Kik Lodge

Girlfriend One was erratic with eggs. One Sunday they'd be spot on, another an embarrassment. I'm not saying Dad asked her to leave because of this. She was a relentless chatterbox and got hiccoughs constantly.

'I like my yolk spoonable,' he said to Girlfriend Two, 'my white firm.' But her eggs were always hard-boiled. Her and Dad used to make pig noises when they laughed, then she went abroad.

Girlfriend Three said she didn't trust boiled eggs. 'Too bloody mysterious for me,' she said, and Dad said nothing. She cooked us fried eggs 'because I can see what's what', and the three of us ate them in silence.

Then Girlfriend Four came along and used a timer, and the result was a perfectly boiled egg, but I knew Dad thought 'cheat'. Last time we saw her, she said, 'Jesus, you two.'

Dad's the one who makes eggs now because Girlfriend Five is vegan, and yesterday he spoke about Mum's eggs.

How the shell would never be hot but warm. How the buttered soldiers would wait in line to be dipped into the yellow squelch. How when I was little, I'd dunk the soldiers and turn them up the other way, watch the yolk trickle down their bodies as far as my fingers.

Girlfriend Five dresses the soldiers now, not with real butter but with apple cider vinegar and almond milk, and I tell her it's different, but it's really very good, because I mean it.

Throwing Her to the Wolves
Susan Carey

The train pulls into Gloucester Station. Taxi money is folded in my pocket to take me to student digs when I arrive at Paddington. Doorstep sandwiches bulge in a paper bag in my rucksack. In the kitchen this morning Mum had just looked on, letting Dad slice the bread. His hands more used to knocking in fence posts or delivering calves than making fiddly sandwiches. I saved a crust that fell on the floor for Bess and gave it to her outside. When we drew off in the Land Rover, instead of barking, she whined. Seemed to know this was a different sort of leaving.

I kiss them goodbye as if I do this sort of thing every day. Say I'll be home at the weekend. Wherever home is now. In the train, I take a seat opposite a woman with her child and look through the window at Mum and Dad standing there. They are out of place on the platform. Country people, not used to the urban activity of a train station. I ache for them. At home, Dad's presence fills the farmhouse kitchen, even when he dozes on the stiff wooden chair in front the Rayburn. For the first time ever, he looks slight, fragile.

I take off my coat and put it on the rack. My breath steams up the window, and I wipe a section clean with my sleeve. My family are framed now, the condensation forming tears I refuse to shed. It's hard enough for everyone without tears. Besides, we are farming people, stoical. A shred of my parents' conversation this morning above Radio 4's Farming Today revealed what Dad truly thought. *Throwing her to the wolves.*

The train moves off and my parents get smaller and smaller. I don't wave them out of sight as Mum always told me that was bad luck and you'd never see that person again. Soon, I will cross the Severn Bridge, and I'll think of what future awaits me while I listen to the beat of the train wheels. *Gotta go, gotta go, gotta go.*

What Bach Tastes Like
Tonia Markou

Bach's music tastes like my mother's *kourabiedes* – Greek butter cookies, sweet and crumbly, sprinkled with powdered sugar on top.

Cookies on my tongue, mother on my mind, I open the closet door. The clothes smell of her. I grab a swallow-patterned blouse, breathe in. Now my lungs do too.

Outside the apartment, ambulance sirens blare through the quiet neighborhood, disrupting my mother's playlist.

Bach's *Aria* fades, and Beethoven's *Moonlight Sonata* begins; melancholy and hope chasing each other with every keystroke. The lemony taste of chicken soup fills my mouth. '*It has superpowers,*' Mom once told me, and sick eight-year-old me believed her, but deep down I knew that she was the one yielding magic. Why couldn't I nurse her back to health?

The next song starts like a slow stroll through the rain. Mom was listening to Satie's *Gymnopedie No.1* that day, letting it lure her away from us, one playful note at a time. And yet, it tastes of homemade bread, fresh orange-grapefruit juice, home and love.

I turn away from the bed. It's still visible in the mirror but less powerful that way.

More sounds echo from the empty rooms: fresh orange juice, crustless turkey sandwiches, *tsureki* at Easter, *melomakarona* at Christmastime, and fruity Pinot Noir rosé wine on the balcony.

The music stops, the apartment full with stillness. In my arms, my mother's blouse grows heavy. I take another smell and gently put it back inside the closet.

Keys rattle in the front door before it opens. 'Sis, you there?' My brother's sneaker-clad steps come closer. 'I thought you might need a hand.'

Tears will flow when I blink or try to speak, so I don't.

As Matthew cradles me in his older brother arms, Bach makes an appearance again.

'What's that? Sounds nice. We should play it at the funeral. She'd like that, don't you think?'

I gulp down the pain. 'It's my favorite Bach symphony.' I look up at him. 'Do you remember Mom's homemade strawberry jam?'

He nods.

'A little too soft and too sweet. That's what it tastes like.'

Our reflections in the mirror manage a smile.

Periscope Portuguesa
D M O'Connor

The Way There

Moored off Muscat, Alfonso de Albuquerque weighed pearls, entered inky figures into conquest chronicles, leaning columns cataloguing greed, and wondered whether to boil or fry the glassfish for lunch. Low on oil, brandy, joy, patience, and citrus, the crew had been mumbling mutiny since Mombasa. Only battle and pillage elevate spirits. Doldrums fanned bloodthirst, still water since Maputo, rowing Galleons inspired nobody. *We need a temple to torch, cannonballs flying, night screams, more slaves.* He tossed the shucked shells onto the staghorn reef, glowing luminescent.

The Way Here

Rounding the Horn, Nelson Setubal maintains the oak was eaten from within by termites, perhaps maggots. Only the Broadnosed Seven Gill Cow Shark knows best—all that infesting pays well. The Puffadder Shyshark might add two-clarifying-cents if found and persuaded to rat. The Houndshark took the fifth when pressed spoke in tongues. Fin envy remained the official gloss for capsize. Overload and tidal misreading were also footnoted. At least that's what Sad Nuno the Cartographer feathered in the dispatch to Henry the Navigator, who well knew attention was propaganda.

Bounty's Privilege

Jackie and Truman sipped breakfast gimlets on the Palácio da Comenda veranda, *would you just look at those Sado sandbars, they seem to be floating,* he said, waving the wand-like cigarette holder. *Aren't we all? Aristotle says cuttlefish are good for circulation. Shall we take the mules up to the windmill later? Conceivably, if I phone my words in on time, and you provide your houseboy's companionship. Truman, you really are a hound. I prefer the word harpy.* A single ripe olive plopped onto a cobblestone. Truman lit Jackie's, and Jackie lit Truman's, not half a worry between them. Ashes flicked out to sea.

Turtle on the Dotted Line
Rosaleen Lynch

The turtle and I form a procession of two in the middle of the road, on the dotted line, heel to toe, following the white dash of paint, the black tarmac space, saying cut along here, timing my step, one, and wait for it, two, balancing plastic bags in both hands, cutting into palms, cars sweeping by on either side. Can't tell a Food Bank if they give you too much to carry, and here's some advice – leave your bags on the kerb if you're chasing anything but the world turtle, she could carry the weight of the world for you.

I was seven when I found a turtle under the caravan that Mam said was my pet, said she got from a rescue centre, though she hadn't left the caravan during daytime in months. She complained it barked too loud, but when men came to visit, gave me money to buy it dog food. I called the turtle Lassie and collected snails in a bucket, feeding them dumpster scraps and testing them for poison with broken jars of peanut butter. If they lived, they became turtle food. I spent the money on human food for me. Then papers got signed, half left at the hospital with Mam and half pinned to my coat with my new address.

The turtle on the road looks like Lassie, but the shell's still intact. I follow as it turns off the broken white line into oncoming traffic, ignoring beeping, swerves and the driver of the grey Volkswagen, who rolls down his window, waiting for me, as he says, to get the fuck out of the way. I step between the car and turtle, and ask the man if he'd like some soup for his troubles, that I have minestrone, tomato or vegetable in cans, and they're heavy, won't replace the energy spent carrying them, or maybe that's celery, and I drop my bags, another defence between man and turtle, put my hands on the bonnet of the car, curved like a shell, warm and vibrating. Is there a beating heart in there? I ask. I think there is, I think there is.

Queen of Hearts
Meili Kaneshiro

Your flippered feet kick and your gloved hands circle and you are doing this to stay still.

Your headlight illuminates the creature in front of you – an alien, yellow eyes and purplish skin and more tentacles than you can see. She is at home here, and you are not. She is suspended without effort, and her sticky fingers move in and out of your narrow cone of vision. You know there should be eight because that's what *octo* means, but there must be more than that – hundreds, possibly.

She could, if she wanted, wrap one of those tentacles around your torso and squeeze. Your delicate organs, already under pressure, would pop. Bones turned to fine flour.

'Follow the card,' she says. And the intricate red designs on the backs blur and seem to move, to change, as her tentacles swipe and swirl.

You choose.

She smiles, you think – but her muscles don't work that way.

You imagine that she smiles.

She shows you – The Joker.

The dark darkens, and even though you shouldn't be able to tell, through your rubbery second skin, the ink is warm.

You'll never find the Queen of Hearts again.

Last Call
Karen Crawford

'Friday I'm in Love' is playing on the digital jukebox at the local dive. 'Last call,' you say and slide a shot across the bar before you saunter over. 'Cure fan?' you ask. I nod, my voice stuck somewhere between your bad boy hair and all-American jaw.

I'm struck by the way your eyes sparkle and flame. They draw me in. *Closer.* Your five o'clock shadow sandpapers my face. *Closer.* Your lips steam up the lenses of my glasses. *Closer.*

I want to be your last call. I'm suddenly jealous of all the last calls that came before.

~

'Saturday Sun' is the song you're humming as you wipe down the bar. You remove your skinny tie and wrap it like a headband around my long wavy hair.

'You're hot,' you say. *Softer.* 'I'm not,' I whisper. *Closer.*

With my contacts in, it's clear – I'm your new last call. We knock back tequila and sway to Crowded House. 'Let's drive to the beach and watch the sunrise,' you say. *Softer.* I shake my head and point towards the bottle. *Closer.* You press your smooth skin against my face. *Softer.*

Your lips cloud my vision.

~

'Sunday Morning' serenades us on Sirius radio. Your phone on the dash starts blowing up, Kelly. Amber. Tiffany. You reach for it. I grab your arm.

Tires swerve, the car rolls, glass shatters. *Louder.* Blood blossoms like an inkblot through the tie still wrapped around my forehead. *Closer.* The sun bleeds upside down on the horizon. *Farther.*

My seatbelt imprisons my chest. *Closer.* I can't feel my fingers to release it. *Farther.* I see three of you lying on the side of the road. I blink you into focus. *Closer.* Your phone falls from your outstretched hand. *Farther.*

A siren hurtles along a desolate highway. *Louder.* The blur of approaching red lights is blinding. *Closer.* Maroon 5 on repeat in my head. *Louder.* Where's my phone? I swear I hear it ringing. *Louder.* I feel a dizzying rush at the sing-song alert of a voicemail. It keeps pinging. *Louder.* My heart pounds. *Louder.* Afraid I'm your last call. *Louder. Louder. Louder.*

River of Leaves
Fiona McKay

It was after a period of exceptionally heavy rain that the floor began to buckle in the sitting room, off to one side of the sofa. We ignored it initially; each perhaps hoping that it was something temporary, something merely warped. If we were surprised when the first shoots came through between the floorboards, we didn't say. We may have thought the sensible thing would be to snip off the branches as they sprouted, yet we didn't, just making little accommodations along the way: small things. One of us moved the sofa a little to the left; one moved the TV a smidgen to the right, so we could continue laughing at our game shows, crying at romances, and biting our nails during the finales of reality TV series to see who gets booted off the island or gets to keep the girl.

We had to remember it was there, and walk around it, which was all fine before the leaves came out, and at first it was fun to watch it out of the corner of our eyes, letting slip a tiny gasp each time a leaf unfurled. It wasn't a major problem, as branches drooped lower under the weight of the leaves.

When autumn came, a rush of wind caused the browned and withered leaves to fall and move around the room in drifts, and we each took our turn to slip in uncareful moments, and though we didn't say so, we all felt it had become a hazard. We could have swept up the leaves, and yet we didn't, and maybe because it was easier to see the TV again once the leaves had fallen, we just let it be.

When spring came, there was a period of furious growth, and the branches extended up towards, and then through, the ceiling. We were definitely alarmed then and rushed up the stairs to assess the damage. When we found the cradle, empty and broken, we stared at each other, unspoken words stopping our mouths, unshed tears clouding our eyes. There was nothing we could do then and nothing left to say. It was too late. All too late.

Pathways
Johanna Robinson

The stranger extracts a pen from his shirt pocket and pats himself for paper. I hand him a scrap of mine.

'You don't know how to get there?'

I shrug. 'I feel like I should remember, but...'

He draws a series of lines. Junctions. A circle.

'That's a hangman,' I tell him, and he stares at me. We both look down the road, one way, then the other. I wonder which direction is noose, which is feet. The street is crawling with people.

He stabs dots into the paper, around the *H* he's drawn. 'You can't miss it.'

I take the stick-figure sketch, hoping he's added a face to the circle, but he's only written: roundabout.

I choose the arm, stuck out at an acute angle, and begin to walk. At the elbow, there's an alley where we used to smoke and drink and shelter – clogged with rubbish now and oozing puddles. I keep going, expecting more, but find only the stump of a dead-end. I turn the directions upside down, retrace my steps. Memories surface, skitter like leaves: a girl, a house, a bag, a bench, another house. Back on the main road, I pause at a grubby window, my face turned ghost by the net curtain. I cough, bring up stuff that should be kept inside, and head for the roundabout.

I cross the choked road, tarmac warmth seeping into the soles of my feet. *I remember sand between toes.* On the other side, I drift between neat, weedless beds, the spring flowers laid out in exuberant designs. *I remember Nan's floral carpets.* Under the soil, I suppose more bulbs are waiting. I lie down on a strip of grass; soon the insects will tickle up my limbs. *I remember Mum's fingers.*

At last, I rise and see that there is a face, after all.

The man extracts a pen from his shirt pocket and pats his spotless white coat for paper. I offer mine, crumpled, stick man, stuck man, lying man, dying man. He takes it, and my hand. Although it's dark now, the streets are alive, endless, pulsing, skittering with memories.

Arrived.

Flooded Valley
Julie Evans

A man with a cauliflower ear unfolds his maps and plans in the tin-roofed village hall. He explains how the valley will flood. It will all be gone – the Hall, the church, the school. Each and every cottage.

'You'll be better off in the new place,' he says. 'Indoor lavvies. Electricity!'

Maggie thinks of the oak tree in her garden, of the woodpeckers that nest there. She thinks of her cottage home, the footprints worn into the flagstone floor, the iron hooks driven into the fireplace lintel for generations of drying drawers and Christmas stockings.

On the day they come with the truck, she scours her front step with a donkey stone that the rag-and-bone man gave her in exchange for Jim's old overalls.

The neighbours laugh. 'What's the point, Maggie, love?'

She purses her lips and carries on. When her step is creamy and immaculate, she stands and looks out across the moor, at the slopes dotted with craggy ewes and purpled with mist-damp heather.

From the back of the truck, as she rattles away, she sees the diggers in the churchyard, excavating Jim from his grave. He's been in there scarce a year. They'll put him in a nice, neat municipal plot on the edge of town, they say. But the soil there will have no scent and no secrets, no stories to tell, no grandfather-bones.

The village slowly becomes a reservoir, a sheet of aqueous blue. The steeple is left as memento, finger-thrusting out from the water, but they take it down when little boys swim out and try to climb its sheer sides. Still, at night, the villagers in their bungalows miles away swear they can hear the muffled sound of the bell calling them from beneath.

In a drought, you can walk through the main street again, a de-molished melancholia of path, broken chimney pot, the arched stones of an ancient bridge.

Listen. Listen hard above the wind. For the chant of times tables from the village school, the whistle of a copper kettle, the ghost-ring of a blacksmith's anvil on the valley wall.

And look. For a front step. Scoured.

In the Night, I Hold My Breath
Heather McQuillan

Sometimes, my mother is a trapeze artist, wearing a tutu of sequinned lace, spectacular when she climbs into the spotlight going so high. She blows a kiss to brush my cheeks. I hold my breath when she drops, sigh with relief when she rises again. Sometimes, she takes so long between the down and the up I think I'll faint from lack of oxygen. Then she flutters her eyelashes to tickle my face goodnight. Silly Billy, she whispers when I cling. Sometimes, my mother dances; the beat pulses up through the dusty floor to shake her to the ends of her hair. Her legs are thin, arms pink–blue with veins, ribs so like chicken bones I wonder how they don't shatter from the throb of her heart. Sometimes, my night-moth mother sleeps late, her powdery wings tattered and torn from slamming against light. When she wakes, her eyes all smudged mascara, she needs heaped spoonfuls of coffee in her cup, just a few minutes more, before I open the curtains. Sometimes, my father says it's all her fault, getting up so high and then crying back to us when she falls. He slams the door in her face. He slams her face in the door. Sometimes, in the dark I hear the thumps and then the long, loud silence. I wait, the breath stoppered in my chest, hungering for a goodnight eyelash kiss.

Morning Bird
Beth Shelburne

The steel door of my cell rattles with the crack of thunder. I feel it from every direction, reminding me there is a whole moving universe outside this place.

I glance out the window, the view of my small world brown and wet. I don't see my favorite bird this morning, the sweetest little thing. She's the color of cigarette ash with orange eyes. The first time I spotted her on the brick windowsill, she looked like a piece of art, still as a painting outside my ratty cage.

When I crank my window open, I can get a few fingers out to drop breadcrumbs on the sill. She pecks away at the crumbs and carries a few away. I like to picture her feeding baby birds, being a good mama. I hope she'll eventually let me touch her. I bet her feathers feel soft as silk. I like the idea of touching a living thing that isn't afraid of me.

I worry that she might meet the stray cats that slink around the yard, skinny and skittish, a hungry look in their eyes. Some of the men have been feeding tuna to the cats. When I get my hands on a pouch of tuna, I eat every flake. I like knowing I'm eating a fish that swam in an ocean far away.

The cats wait for all the guys to leave the yard and then creep over, gobble up the tuna and run away to the scrubby woods that surround this place. When they first brought me here, I looked out the van window as tattered-looking pines and shrubs whizzed by. Once inside the prison, there are no green plants or trees, no flowers, only the yard with dry grass the color of straw.

My bird is like a tiny miracle. The best part is giving an unexpected treat to another creature of the world. What do they call it? Generosity. Never thought much until now about how it might feel good to do something nice for someone, even if that someone is just a grey, nameless bird who stops by on some beautiful mornings.

Imprisoned Lightning
Katherine Gleason

Bring me your tired, your poor, your huddled masses – but now I need an espresso and a pair of sensible shoes. The first one hundred years were fun. I still get a kick out of ticker-tape parades. I've even come to enjoy the odd rituals – mobs of visiting school children, cylinders of animal flesh crammed into bread and mouths, the booms and colored sparks that fan over the harbor on a summer's eve.

Now, though, my world is shrinking. I've got sores and blisters. I need to break free of this metal cage. I am not this vessel, this green shell. I am Rivka, who fled pogroms and an arranged marriage. I am Samuel, who followed the constellations north and toiled to buy Sally's freedom. I am Miguel and Juana searching for water at the southern border. I am Elizabeth and Lucretia and Susan and Harriot, Alice and Lucy, Frederick and Ida. I am Marsha, who may or may not have thrown a shot glass and started a riot that launched a movement.

I will not be reduced to this object, monumental though it be. No one can pack me inside, lock me up. I am not your symbol, logo, snow globe. I am the Mississippi, Ohio, Allegheny. I am the Colorado, Snake, and Rio Grande. I am the wind shearing off the Rockies. I am a sequoia, giant redwood, prickly pear, arms extended, blooming in the April sun.

We have work to do. Yes, I'm talking to you. First thing, I'm putting down this torch and dipping my feet in the ocean. If the current's not too strong, I'll take a swim. Please join me. Then it's a meeting of the minds, a working vacation in Nashville to consult with Athena. We may even zip up to Niagara Falls for some inspiration.

Know that you are electric. Let's raise the wattage. I want to hear you roar. Get me that coffee, never mind about the shoes. Make sure you vote and bring me a screwdriver.

Come now, hurry. It's time to go.

The Fall
David O Dwyer

Pillar Brae. The slop of brown porter on a polished counter. The cream-moustache above my father's lips.

A gut feeling. Pillar Brae.

Late April, the sun in Taurus. There's nothing much going on in school, so my brother Dec convinces Dad to bring us.

Pillar Brae. A song like a bird, royal blue-and-gold richness of the jockey's silks.

'Come on, the Brae.'

I think of a donkey. I see an orange bag of King Crisps an old man grabs from a bar girl. I hear the crumple.

I'd like to taste salt, but Dec pulls me away.

He doesn't say it to Dad. He wants this for his own, a special win.

~

As soon as they turn into the home stretch, sparks flying, whips swishing, Dec's face reddens. He grabs the rails.

She's leading the pack. At the last fence, she jumps but twists in mid-air, an eye aghast, a mouth foaming, the legs splayed. I don't know whether she has jumped too soon or has something happened to her? She hits the fence; the jockey is slung across grass.

Pillar Brae is on the ground. Pillar broken. Her chestnut coat sparkles with sweat. The jockey is stretchered away to indistinguishable sounds.

The rest of the pack gallop by. Colourspin.

A man in a wax jacket gets out of a jeep. Produces from a leather bag a gun and a horn. I grab Dec's arm. The screwing of the silencer horn on the gun is prolonged and harsh, like the caw of a demented crow. The shot pops. There's a flapping of wings as Pillar Brae's hind legs rise and fall.

'I don't care if she's dead,' Dan squirms, walking ahead. 'I'll have to ask Dad for more money now.'

Sweet smell of pipe tobacco. Horse dung. Cherrywood, the light fading.

That afternoon, I thought of the randomness of a coin spinning. The uniqueness of gold sought as drinks and money are exchanged. The gnarled hands of a grandfather. Things passed down. Rope uncoiled as Dec left us years later. In my head again and again and again. The randomness of the fall.

Clipped
Jo Dixon

The days he is disturbed by Uncle's phone call are functional. The last time Uncle called, he queued for a washer behind his neighbour, watched him fishing about in his jeans' pockets, offered him a clutch of coins, explained the change machine wasn't working. The neighbour banged against his shoulder, breaking for the door. Uncle hasn't called. He gathers brush, paper, ink and inkstone from the drawer in the roll-top desk. He waits for the sun.

A fist slams against his window. The frame shakes. The venetian blind jerks. He squares a sheet of paper on the desk pad under four weights. The sun lays its first stripe on the carpet, and he pulls the cord. The blind rattles up. His neighbour, sent home before the shift has even started, spits consonants at the glass. The half-brick slashes his cheek. A stroke of red pours into the corner of his mouth. And the brush responds to his touch: black lines with the energy of birds' wings.

At rush hour, the road is empty. The traffic lights repeat themselves uninterrupted. He flies out of his front door, crouches on the tarmac, inks the white centreline. Everyone's at home.

When to Release
Abbie Barker

Dad gave Owen a plush football for his third birthday and taught him how to tackle. They stomped around the living room, stances wide, chests forward. *My little linebacker*, Dad called him, *my defensive end*. When I joined in, the game fizzled. Dad shielded me from Owen's jabs, worried I'd rip my dress or bruise my elbows. I waited until no one was looking and squished that football between couch cushions, buried it under beds. Somehow, Dad always found it.

In middle school, I begged Dad to teach me to throw a spiral. Beneath the backyard pines, he showed me how to step into the throw and when to release. As he rescued the ball from the dirt and fetched wobbly spirals from the wrong side of the fence, Dad asked if we should stop, if I had homework. Even when I said no, he'd retreat into the den to watch a game. I'd hover in the doorway while he spoke to Owen in a language I didn't understand.

Later, I met Owen in pubs. This was after the injury, after he and Dad stopped talking. This was when he was thick and sad, eyes fixed on a row of muted screens, stacking empties by the lip of the bar. Owen sold life insurance. He spent an hour in the gym every day. Sometimes he asked about Dad, and I told him about the ball he kept near his bed, how he held his hands open across his chest like he was waiting for a pass. Dad called me every week. He wanted to talk about football, but in a way I'd understand. He said the game changes you when you let it. I still don't know if he believed anyone should let it.

The Supermarket Is Made for Scalping Sprouts
Marilyn Hope

Hair today, gone tomorrow, says Wachts via razor. He rehearsed for weeks in the produce storeroom, stroking apricots free of vellus with a disposable blade. Thank God for the practice: Teddy's scalp is the tenderest of territories, and the boys are crammed Lucas-Ben-Sam in the bathtub to see who'll start bleeding first. Wachts chases the curve of Teddy's neck in steady columns. A thousand fruits and vegetables sitting bald in their sale bins. By now, not even the onions make him cry.

'Occipital,' says Doctor Ben, naming the proper bone each time Wachts braces his fingertips somewhere on Teddy's head. 'That's the parietal, I think. Do you feel the eminence?'

By a different definition. Teddy asked Wachts by phone, voice weak beneath the deli neons. *It's A.L.L. official now.* Cancer joke, funnier with the hand motions. *Could you do it for me? You're the only one who won't be an adult about it.*

You can trust me not to start sobbing, is what you mean, said Wachts.

Teddy laughed like dry leaves. *That's what I said.*

They'd celebrated his birthday in the hospital that April, prednisone and party hats, fourteen candles he couldn't blow out. Lucas made dominos out of tongue depressors, and their fingers were filled with splinters by the time they laid down their last doublets.

Now, in the bathroom, they're all five thinking the same few things. Sam dabs Teddy's cheek with a tissue.

'Zygomatic,' says Ben.

'Looking good,' says Lucas. 'Really.'

Teddy touches his almost-bare scalp. 'Just finish.'

Wachts readies the razor again, still thinking about apricots. He wonders if the whole world's built on this sort of dichotomy. Today, Wachts has a steady hand and queasy heart. Today, Teddy's eyes are drying, but his head is weeping curls.

Going
Jude Hayland

You must have left at speed.

It explains the forgotten socks. Two crisp shirts still insisting on their space. That scarlet sweater.

In the bathroom, there's the faintest trace of bristle on the basin. The floor tiles are still wet from water that puddled around your feet. A damp towel loops at half-mast.

So you are not entirely gone. In spite of the words you wrote.

Funny, I would have expected more than a cowardly scurrying away. That absenting note in the hall.

Perhaps you were pleased by the pert, pretty phrases, thought them kind. Or at least not too unkind. Knowing I would read them endlessly, ferret into their roots, trace their cadences.

Already it is dark. Dregs of a November day. I wear those two white shirts of yours, button both up, straitjacket like, but there is no comfort in their cleanliness. You have been washed from them, laundered out, leaving me no trace.

But the scarlet sweater provides.

I bury my face in its folds, find your scent, your very self in the soft wool, smother it with my tears. The wool swiftly grows sodden.

I move from room to room, disorientated. The reason for each hour suddenly bewilders, and I am without any compass. I yearn for your key in the door and wonder at the absurdity of it all.

At me loving you. Inordinately.

At you, merely amused, diverted, placated for a while by my charms, my looks, possibly even my mind.

Until it became prosaic for you, insufficiently sufficient. Or so your note says.

So here I am, victim of your vagaries, but mostly of my own blind passion, a stubborn refusal to see with clarity.

But my eyes are open now (or will be once this appalling weeping stills), and I'm grateful for your brutal honesty. Truly.

Although of course, if you change your mind, it's possible that I, too, will prove fickle to my resolve. Take you back into my arms.

So I will keep those shirts in the wardrobe, the scarlet sweater.

Place forgotten socks in the drawer.

Talismans, if you like, of you.

Of a sufficiency of something called love.

Song for My Father's Funeral
Debra A Daniel

Mother always said I inherited my father's hair. If I wanted movie star hair like she used to have, I'd need to shave and start over.

In truth, she always hated shaved heads, detested my father's crewcut though he never stopped buzzing himself.

Now we're at his funeral. My mother decides to speak. She walks to the podium, dramatically large purse on her arm, a captured hanky fluttering in her hand.

She begins revealing all my father's indiscretions. In kaleidoscopic detail. Details she knows. Or exaggerates. Or invents.

She riffs. My mother, the stand-up comic of death.

'My husband was so unfaithful...'

'How unfaithful was he?' the mourners holler in unison.

She answers. Listing names. Alphabetically.

'If this service were in a respectable church,' she says, 'I wouldn't be talking about cheap women with lipstick too red to be believable. Red lipstick is ab-whore-nt. Get it? Ab-whore-nt. And too much red lipstick has congregated in this room right now.'

Then she dares anyone who ever screwed her husband to stand up.

'Red lipstick would be banished in church, but this ain't no church. It's a poor excuse of a funeral home for a poor excuse of a husband. So put your hands together for the grieving widow.'

She opens her purse, pulls out a wig, and plops it on her head. Glorious dark movie star hair. My mother, like a smoky-voiced jazz club torch singer, grabs the microphone and belts out the blues. Gritty lyrics about jilted wives. Brassy floozies. Low-class crewcuts. Bumpy scalps of worthless no-good loser men.

When my starlet-haired mother finishes, she exits. Everyone follows until no one is left but me. I bow my head, bury my fingers in the memory of my father's hair.

He Is Forty. He Is in His Sock Drawer. He Hesitates
Tom Browning

Of all days, birthdays are when you wear your best socks. The best are comfortable and allow your feet to breathe. But it is also the quarter-final, and he must follow his intuition when choosing. As always, Tim and Ali will mock his superstition whilst watching the game in the pub.

The others will join later. They will celebrate with a meal and a few drinks.

Those without children will have dogs.

They will need to leave.

He looks at a frayed navy seam and knows it's silly to choose socks with holes in. *That's more hole than sock*, he hears his grandmother say in teasing tones of unconditional love. Her voice rings clear as it did when she was alive. It is not superstition. He must give something to the team, give something of himself away.

He'd tried to hide it from Leila, but she soon twigged. She said his compromise showed *a beautiful potential*, and for years she encouraged him, squeezing him tight, grinning over his shoulder as he talked through the tatty options. It wasn't superstition. He really did feel a connection, a sensitivity to the possible outcomes that extended, diverging from every pair. A thrill haemorrhaging free from the suffocation of holding someone close: it was enough.

And then, it wasn't. It was pants and shirts and *can't you dress nice just for me?*

Can't you miss the game, so we can have the day?

Why can't you give more?

Why couldn't he?

Standing at the chest of drawers, he can't decide – tries to hear how he narrated his options to Leila. Then he sees the time... *Fuck it.* He grabs a barely-worn mustard sock. Its baby-soft wool caresses the thrust of his freshly washed foot. He is already reaching for its pair when he hears a static-like crackle – feels the air rushing in.

He looks down.

There's his pale big toe, yellow threads tight around its knuckle.

Now drops of water splattering its nail.

They soak into the wool.

He feels one hand

clenching tight.

The other, trembling, snatches a fistful of socks and stuffs them into his mouth.

A Penguin in Dust-Bowl Town
Sharon Boyle

As she walks, she remembers the *Ford Escape* with its pale blue chassis that mirrored the wide, open skies. There had been no shelter inside the car – oven-hot, she'd been breathless and clammy, staring out at a vista of rust-coloured clay baked into fissures.

There's been no shelter either from the snippy-tongued gossips who think it fine to snark out comments about her pinafore and sandals. She is meant to overhear their words. *The way she slaps, slaps about the place like a penguin.*

She would love to see a penguin up close. Of course, it would die within the hour in this listless, linear place where anything respectable is nailed onto the High Street and where every house reeks of the piggeries.

The only pleasant smell, apart from the perfume women use to mask their glow, is the mix of oranges and biscuits that fill the school dinner-hall at snack time. School is a safe place where the teachers do their best not to judge.

She scuffs up the long path to Don Fleming's house that squats on the edge of town, ignoring the crow that swipes its beak in the dust.

Back, back, it caws.

She wants to agree. *You're so right, I should*, but her family has spoken of shame – mostly theirs.

Behind a wire-netted enclosure, Don Fleming's dog barks crazily. They say folk choose pets based on themselves, in which case Don Fleming is wiry and dangerous.

She didn't want to come here, to walk along the path, to be warned by the crow, to be greeted by the dog, to remember the blue car where she gave herself to the boy who spoke of togetherness and foreverness. But here she is, her and the baby bump, finding the only shelter they can.

Running Boy
Marianne Rogoff

(Inspired By The Photograph By Manuel Alvarez Bravo.)

Felipe runs because he can. His mother sits still in a downtown doorway with her hand out all day long, for as far back as he can remember. He was born in a doorway and lives there with her.

He has left her behind, three blocks back. He knows these streets, bumps in the stones. The boy is small but feels himself growing. He sees grown men, how hard they work and what will be asked of him, what is being asked of him now.

He hoists high a box of tiny painted wood turtles with bobbing heads. *One peso, one peso.* When he reaches the plaza, he lowers them and holds them out. *One peso* for these miniature toys that make the *gringos* smile. They stroke the glossy paint, say, *no gracias.* He pushes the box closer. *One peso.* A very small amount. You touch the *chingón tortuga*, you hand me a fucking *peso.* He knows that prime time is after coffee when tourist pockets are full of change. He presses the *gringo's* knees until the man sighs and reaches for two coins, just to make him go away.

Felipe had a late start this morning. Sunlight reached the doorway and warmed him and the body of his mother to stay asleep, wrapped in their wool blanket, gold with bright red, black, white connecting triangles. Overnight he lies awake in cold moonlight tracing fingertips over the lines. This journey through the weaving comforts him as the path leads back each time to where he started.

Today, he and his mother have eaten two tortillas each with a spoonful of beans from the corner vendor and shared an orange the man was about to throw away. Felipe makes himself a promise now: *one peso* in the left pocket for *Jefe, one* in the right pocket for *Madre*, and if I am lucky to earn *one peso* more, I put it in my sock. He will hoard coins in this way until he's a man, with enough to buy a place for *Madre* and him to live behind a doorway they can close against nights when there is no moon.

Small and Stillborn
Lydia Kim

I call her my mother because they cut me out of her.

Like all mothers, it took a long time to learn how to orbit her, how to hold her, which parts were safe, which ones were like bad weather. How to tell when she's come unsheathed. She doesn't slice, she stabs. My mother disembowels both of her children with one sentence and then turns and cuts the fruit away from the rind, peeling it from the pith with precision, serving it up, toothpicks inserted into the center of each glistening chunk. The human head is full of rinds and piths, did you know? The tough, pocked outer layer, stinking of sebum, the softer, bitter fascia underneath, the motherboard of nerves and arteries, rubbery with persistence. You really have to get in there.

My mother trained me with the old ways. Whispers, pinches, things that need close inches, not good aim. I liked it. How I could see their certainty fading as they slinked away, knowing they'd never return and never forget. I haven't been made once since reaching middle age, outside the narrow cone of viability for women. I could be anyone, the crone, housekeeping, a first wife. That's Occam's razor. The simplest explanation is usually the truth: he died of a self-inflicted cut. (He asked for it.)

My mother skins quickly, revealing the quivering freshness underneath. She taught me how to appear suddenly, how bloodless things are when surprise chokes the flow. How to walk away without looking back. (The antidote to remorse is confidence.) Who deserved it, who is acceptable collateral damage. I think she may be proud of me, the dexterity I've developed to wield her expertly, even against myself. On lonely days I bring her forth for a bit of bloodletting, running her against the surface tension of other people's happiness. She's with me when I sleep, my hand tight around the mother of pearl handle, the good part stabbed into the floor.

She's a short and peaked, my mother, the length of a finger, the width of a thumb. She doesn't bend, she's easily hidden. She doesn't, like a sword, sing.

Forget Meringues
Bronwen Griffiths

She said – *you'll slip down the plug-hole, you're thin as a rake. For not eating your greens, the pork pie, the charming rice pudding.*

I said – *I eat baked beans, raw oats, Marmite fingers, fruit jelly, brandy snaps with cream, Angel Delight whisked up into clouds, meringues light as feathers. Is that not enough?*

I will be light as a feather, a cloud, a meringue. I will sail across the sky unfettered from fractions, fatty pork pies, slug-throwing boys and snappy dogs. Unfettered from stodgy rice pudding, sloppy greens and sensible brown shoes.

Yet curves arrive with thighs that spread, chubby cheeks and breasts Garry Rowlands tries to grab.

I *will not* have curves.

Forget meringues, brandy snaps with cream, buttery Marmite fingers. Think Ryvita and one slice of cucumber. Think water from the tap. Think jutting hip-bones and bathroom scales. Think dark corners, passive resistance; silence.

The weight falls away. No one asks. No one says a word.

One night I awake ravenous for the full moon and the bite of chair legs. When I sleep, I dream brandy snaps and cream, buttery toast, meringues, jelly, Angel Delight, slices of cheese. I dream lemon sponge, chocolate digestives and thick-cut marmalade.

My scapulae stick out like wings, my belly button pushes up through skin like a broken doorbell. I fall in love with my hip bones and the flat of my stomach. I slip down the plug-hole, I fall through glass, I stop bleeding; I do not eat.

As we stroll through the streets of Stourbridge during a twenty-four-hour sponsored starve-in to raise money for Oxfam, my eyes devour the cream cakes in Cranage's windows. They gulp the frothy coffee at Guggs' and swallow the packets of broken biscuits at Woolworth's.

Nothing passes my lips.

When the starve-in is complete, I am undone by Mrs Twomey's curry. I request second helpings.

Suddenly I desire curves.

Passing By
Em Kinnear

Sometimes I pass by myself – still waiting on cracked tarmac, outside the old hospital wing, leaning against crumbling red walls, slumped on the ground, on a bench, head-in-hands, eyes-to-the-sky. Nighttime becomes a breeze, a freezing wind, spitting rain.

Afterwards, I walk, sometimes all day, between wilting cornfields, winding through old forests, ivy curved around trunks, treading over a sea of moss, I trail on. Eventually earth breaks away into gritty sand, and I work my way over clumpy dunes, fill my lungs with briny air.

As the tide pulls out, I hide crabs beneath rocks, survey the horizon – could I swim to the islands, see the nesting puffins?

In the scratchy dusk, musty fires flare inside speckled cottages, dusty yellow light thins, tiredness overcomes me, but I wait, just a little longer.

Often at night, she reappears with ten stubby toes, a tiny snub nose, eyes which never opened but must have been grey-blue, but her mottled skin is always turning. I see soft baby grows, little cream socks and an empty cot.

Sometimes, I pass by myself in the bustling city streets, hiking up hillsides, or sleeping on a train – waiting with generations of mothers who lactated, contracted and bled, who never held their babies.

Waiting
Not nine months
But many lifetimes.

Mine?
E A Colquitt

It's been a while since she first asked him. He still hasn't given her a proper answer, though making the commitment does have its pros. All the sources say a life without such circumstances costs you. Why not dig down and settle – in your home town, too?

He should have known before now, like when he was about to leave on his think-about-it holiday, and she spent *hours* tapping away on her phone when he was *trying* to explain what Bobby liked to play with, what time she woke up, what to feed her. All the important stuff.

And now he's back from that trip, and Bobby lies stone cold on the floor of her cage. There *is* a new one, back in the house: an apology present. But it's not the same. Bobby II is no canary. *He's* a scarlet *macaw*.

The real Bobby and her humans are in the garden, saying goodbye. They bury her, cage and all, winching it down into a pit in the once-pristine lawn – which he, of course, agreed to dig, but only as long as *she* did the covering-over part.

And she does. The earth skitters between the cage bars at first, the metal structure acting as a sort of open coffin, strewn with brown flowers, dust to dust. Then, half-open. Bobby soon disappears. The patch of soil only grows in the middle of the lawn.

After, she lights a cigarette in remembrance; they have no candles. The wind's in the wrong direction, so the smoke goes everywhere, stinging his eyes. It creeps into what's left of the grass, coating the green in grey. Aren't there laws against that kind of thing?

She pauses before taking another drag. 'So,' she asks again, 'have you decided yet? About us?'

His wary eyes meet hers. Actually, he has decided. Maybe he even made up his mind a long time ago.

He doesn't give the go-ahead, of course. He'll be thinking about this day, about Bobby's descent into the earth, for a while to come. And why would you choose a future whose only direction is down?

The New Mattress
Eleonora Balsano

Our twenty-year-old mattress has lost its firmness.

We strip the bed and take one long, last look at it. There are coffee stains along the edges, souvenirs of young weekends of love for breakfast. A heart-shaped, brown blotch on my side from when I started bleeding and our unborn daughter died. The pink, thick smear on the piping from the nail polish I apply when I can't sleep.

At the shop, a man named Edgar lets us try three different types. Do you sleep on your back, on the side – or maybe on your tummy? He asks, patting his own bulging stomach with a knowing grin.

Our anoraks still zipped to our chins, we lie under bright neon lights, holding hands. You squeeze mine and say, will this do? I shrug, mourning for a time when everything felt right.

A woman in a beige trench coat brushes my shoulder with her arm but doesn't say sorry. She asks for a Natural Pocket Sprung 2000, and Edgar slavishly nods.

I wonder if her old mattress is still pristine or if it's soiled, like ours.

Atop a Simple Foam upholstered in Belgian linen, we watch her pay and leave.

In the end, we toss a coin.

On a rainy Tuesday morning, the new mattress arrives in our home, thick and taut and without a past.

That night, bouncing on fresh springs, I dream of the old mattress and our romance carved on it, both soaking wet in some waste sorting centre.

Transformation
Annette Edwards-Hill

In Winter the toenail on Jane's little toe thickened slowly underneath woolly socks. She ignored her feet until it was almost Spring, and she felt her toenails pushing against the end of her boots.

As the days got longer, she abandoned her shoes. The children noticed the nail curling into a narrow claw. The eldest asked her to put shoes on. The youngest screamed when it brushed against his leg.

As Jane's children whined with the boredom of summer holidays, the nail grew longer, the tip getting sharper, until she could use it to scratch her name into the dirt. The youngest cried when the eldest said the claw would rip his heart out if he got too close.

At night Jane escaped. In a dream, from high in a tree, she watched her children run in a field of horses. She swooped then felt a hand on her face. The eldest child stood by the bed. She pointed to blood bubbling from a long scratch on Jane's leg. The claw, a weapon, gleamed like a knife.

The doctor said it was probably fungus. Jane looked at her foot, expecting to see a field of mushrooms. The test came back negative, the claw free of spores. Jane asked the doctor if he knew a good vet.

It got colder, and the trees shed their leaves. When Jane pulled her socks off, she found tiny feathers, a fur on top of her feet.

The youngest showed her pictures of eagles in a book he'd found in the school library. Eagles can fly long distances, he said. They have claws, like your toes.

The toe broke through Jane's socks and then her shoes. She went everywhere in bare feet. The frost burning her heels.

Jane woke at night, the skin on her spine stinging like she'd fallen on thistles. When she touched her back, she found a tiny nub on each shoulder blade.

By the morning, she had wings. She spread her arms. Her wingspan as wide as the eagle in her child's book.

Jane stepped through the open window and flew away.

Miracle at the Zoo
Tonia Markou

Vibrant orange fur hangs off the orangutan like rags from a clothesline; skin grey leather, lips curled upward in a constant smile.

Where are you?

Olivia brushes a finger over her own face, tracing the fine lines around her eyes while searching the compound.

There. A tiny hand clutches tightly at the orangutan's hairy stomach. The mother holds onto the heavy rope, stretches her other arm toward the ground to pick up a dirty mango. She takes a bite. Juice squirts down her mouth, onto her baby's head. Her long pink tongue licks it clean. Gently, she cradles her offspring, and Olivia finds herself humming a lullaby her mom used to sing. A lullaby she was going to sing to her own child.

The animal looks up, eyes dark as onyx stones fixed on Olivia; compassion in their depths. Without warning, the chain-link fence that separates them shimmers. If Olivia focuses long enough, she can almost reach through it, embrace mother and child, breathe in the baby's scent.

'A miracle, isn't it?' A young woman has joined Olivia, her hand drawing circles over her protruding belly the size of a small watermelon.

Olivia's not sure if she means her own miracle or the caged creatures in front of them. Hypnotized by the woman's circular hand motion, Olivia mirrors the action, touching a stomach which never got the chance to grow.

The smell of burnt butter wafts over from the Cott'n'Candy truck and brings a sudden wave of nausea like a phantom pain of a limb long lost.

Footsteps behind her.

'Excuse me, ladies, the zoo closes in about ten minutes.'

Olivia doesn't turn around, afraid to miss a tender glance, a fond caress.

Perched between two branches, baby pressed against her chest, the orangutan studies Olivia as if *she* were the exotic animal.

'I'll be back tomorrow.'

Searching for a Likeness
Tom O'Brien

The photo of you by the cottage door has a faded corner, from years of sunlight through a junk shop window stencilled with the word Antiques. The restorer knows he can fix that.

He rescued the monochrome picture of you in your cinched cotton dress from a box of things you'd recognise; a man's wallet and watch chain, his keys, another man's comb mixed in.

The restorer pours a glass of whiskey, then wipes and smooths the print with a lint-free cloth. He scans it into his laptop, a device you wouldn't recognise, no more than when he changes a TV channel, hears a call go to voicemail, or watches a plane leaving in the evening sky.

But in other ways, your lives are similar. He takes care dressing every day, cleans his apartment, putting things back to how they were, and fills the hours by reading some of the same books as you.

This thing he does with the old pictures is a hobby, not an obsession, he would say, but he finds feelings he has no words for locked away in these old photos.

He adjusts the image of the image of you for contrast, for haze, filters for dust and scratches, but the restorer wants to bring back more than was lost. He wants to bring back what couldn't be captured with the technology of your time.

He searches the picture of you looking at the bird in the hanging cage and finds, reflected in a window, the man who took the photo. How still you stood for him in the long exposure. But from a blur of your hair, the restorer knows there was a breeze, and with that he is with you. He looks through his reflection on the screen and sees the sunlight on your skin, smells the perfume of the flowers you planted, hears the twitter of the bird that looks past you to the sky above, and colours it the palest turquoise blush.

That's the only thing he gets right in this picture of you.

The Woman in the Pink Hoody
Dettra Rose

They say the gallery queue was famous for its slow shuffling, a snake of endless waiting. Street vendors sold warm chestnuts to people bored or hungry enough to buy them at hiked-up prices. Buskers strummed; fire-twirlers spun. Clowns cartwheeled, and all dropped hats to rustle gold and silver.

They say once inside the gallery's glass panes, maps located her portrait. Only one person at a time could enter the temperature-controlled chamber and admire her painting. Even though her face was canvas, oils and pigment, she soothed fury in a storming man and melancholy in a weeping woman.

They say her bronze eyes saw other worlds. She is the painted soul of silvery moonlit rivers.

They say she's trouble – her unclaimable beauty riled men up too much. She looked down on unpainted women and made them feel ugly, cheap and small. She's fake. An ideal. Unreal. One man spat on her – another pulled a knife.

They say her tears bleached the precious antique paint.

They say she had a private letterbox at the gallery. Her guard opened the mail daily; purple and red envelopes. He read her every word.

They say she replied, but that must surely be bullshit.

They say the moon was a pewter newborn arc when she disappeared, the night shadow-dark. Nobody knows how she did it. Nobody knows how she slipped from the canvas onto bustling streets, golden gown trailing.

They say it was her guard – she begged him to cut her from the gilded frame. He's since been arrested and charged. People still queue to see the canvas where she lived. The beautiful shape she left. Her deep lake of calm.

They say I'm lying when I tell them she was walking barefoot, crow feathers in her hair under a hot-pink hoody, collecting raindrops in her cupped palms. She crossed the road to the park, and I followed.

They say she's let everybody down. She's a national treasure – our heritage. She should go back and live in her canvas. From the way she was plucking a mandolin on the bandstand, dancing and drumming with the feral mob, I don't think she will.

Days of Carnival
T L Ransome

The mountain brume was lacquering the piers when I returned. The waterfront was slick, somber with rot, like something they had raised from the Pacific.

And so they had.

The old arcade was closed, so I leaned on a piling worn smooth by the backs of many panhandlers.

I imagined our carousel in drydock. My horse was white and blue; yours was black like the Apocalypse. We gripped the twisted poles like candy sticks and then shot off to the taffy pull. The robot-arms went in and out, round and round. We faced each other in mimicry. Our arms scooped up and down, home and away.

I walked north. Your father's old shop was baptized in fluorescence. Carnations had replaced the zombie comics; keychains supplanted the foam shrunken heads. They'd kept the name, Evergreen Trading Post, but nothing else remained. Nothing of the strange, exotic place we'd haunted while my parents were at work.

Hana behind the counter used to give us mealworms trapped in lollipops. She blasted Metallica from the jukebox as visitors marveled at Bart the many-tailed croc.

Your father popped in and out of the office, smiling, offering advice to tourists. He'd been to Hanoi, Sydney, Lesotho, Rio. He knew the story of everything.

He officiated at our wedding. One calloused hand came down over our small fingers in the sunset. He knew I wanted it to stick.

Twenty years on, I heard it hadn't. Your head, swimming drunk, came down to meet a piling in the dark. Nothing stuck then but the water.

The old arcade was closed, so I stared out across the Sound. The saber-toothed haze of the Olympics held us as we drifted in the gray, watched us going up and down, home and away.

The Dinner Guest
Thomas Malloch
AUTUMN 2021 FIRST PLACE

All day, every day, the stomach gnaw is commanding. So that all that she had once been, becomes Hunger. This Hunger scours for nuts under blasted trees. It turns over stones to see what morsels might be crawling there. It scans the grey, lethargic waves to see what edible dead thing might be carrying to the shore, for there will of course, be nothing live. This Hunger cannot pause for thought. Or it would know. There will be nothing. Except the water flowing off the hill, the colour of potter's slip.

In the night, she hears sausages. Sizzling in the pan, spitting fat. She feels their heat. Sniffs their comfort. Licks her lips. Tastes their grease. She anticipates the bite, the spicy meaty texture, the salt. Then wakes with iron in her mouth. Her jaws have been chewing on nothing but themselves, and scorbutic gums bleed easily. She swallows. She can ill-afford to spit.

And now the urge to urinate. What has taken all day to gather at her ankles re-distributes at night; into the circulation, through the kidneys, dripping down to gather in a distending bladder. The solace of sleep is interrupted, seven times a night.

She steps outside the shack and squats among the rocks, trousers round ankles that are still puffed-up. Eyes close, a momentary beatification at the relief of pressure.

When she opens again, more joy. A single torch bobbing along the coastal path. A dinner guest to greet. She grabs at her trousers and stands.

In her pocket, a blade keens.

Half a Man and a Candle
Annette Edwards-Hill
AUTUMN 2021 SECOND PLACE

After the fire, my brother moved home. Mum didn't say how the fire started, and I didn't ask. I watched Richard move about the house, the ink of skulls, demons and daggers mixing with the melted skin on his arms.

At the river, we swam in the murky water. I stayed away from the edges where the eels sunned themselves. I saw Richard looking at me, casting his eye over the empty canvas of my pale, hairless skin. I hid myself in the water until I could crawl out and cover myself with a towel.

The next morning Richard said we were going for a drive. The tattoo studio was in an old shop down an alleyway. Richard talked to the tattooist, and I looked through a book at images of demons, tigers and bulldogs.

'Have you chosen?' Richard asked. I turned the page and pointed at a medieval scene of a priest in a cave, lit by the flickering light of a candle.

The tattooist raised his eyebrow. 'That will cover your back, what about something smaller. To start with?'

Richard looked at me, a hard line across his forehead, his crossed arms, a mess of ink and burns. Mum's name cut in half with pink skin, a snake head emerging from knots of fire broken skin.

The tattooist started his gun. The noise was an army of bees and then a frenzied feeding of wasps, the needle a burning knife. I imagined it cutting, revealing the bone of my spine.

I gripped the table I lay on, taking deep breaths as the needle lashed my skin, but the scream rose in me. I put my hand over my mouth. I got to my feet and ran.

In the mirror, my back was a landscape of raised black lines. The outline of half a man and a candle.

I didn't swim that summer. At the river, I watched the dark shapes of the eels close to Richard as he floated in the current. I sat on the bank in my T-shirt, the sun hot on my back, the candle etched into my skin on fire.

Domestic Goddess
Kirsteen Ure
AUTUMN 2021 THIRD PLACE

The recipe was ancient, handed down from her mother and hers before. The goddess's tendrils billowed in excitement. She stilled herself and turned her attention to the recipe's instructions, familiar and fashioned from antiquated constellations, stars stitched into ripped squares of adjoining dimensions.

The goddess pulsed her consciousness: released and gathered the right matter, trying not to hurry. Her mother placed a great deal of importance on the right type of languid immortality.

She summoned particles and equipment – a celestially proportioned sieve, particle accelerator (new, in gas-giant orange).

Everything lined up like slices of an aeon. No need, of course, to put time in a line: before, after, little happenings, with no way back. But she found it pleasant – one of her quirks.

Fermions first: sprinkle, stir. Bosons (sifted), next. The batter moved. Colours sparked. Not a moment too soon, she transferred the mix, thick and popping, to her collider.

The batter splashed her tendrils. She wiggled them on the folds of astral fabric covering her matter and consciousness, an apron with tenth dimension pockets. The batter began to expand, and the goddess disappeared from the heat of her own kitchen into another time when her mother had made the same recipe and the little planets were cooling. There, she drew one to her – swirling blue patched with green: wet, salt, wooded crunch.

Heaven.

Her next choice, yellow. She sucked gas and hard-centre through its iced-halos, slipped the leftover ice onto her tendril to make a ring. It dripped as she bit it away.

The crack of ice seemed to echo at her temples when she came back. The mix before her was not quite her mother's. Something had soured. She checked her ingredients, the accelerator settings, then bit into her own green and blue creation: salt slicked with petrochemical tang. Oily, off. She spat. Probabilities fell out of her with the morsel until the problem was clear. She'd left it a million years too long. Enough time for hairless monkeys to foul its surface. They'd turned it, sucked the flavour before she could.

She drew antimatter from her pocket. The soured little thing was no more.

Woodbine
Rosaleen Lynch
AUTUMN 2021 FOURTH PLACE

The window flips and with it the world outside and you say it's an optical illusion, like the young and old woman or the rabbit-duck, just perspective, which I'd agree with, but you weren't even looking, lying in bed, watching the smoke rise from your cigarette instead, knowing I won't kiss you now, but smoking anyway, like the man outside but he's breathing in the smoke, instead of out, and walking backwards, ash catching up with his cigarette, to make it whole again, and the woman he met walks her bike backwards the other way, her lipstick reapplying, from his lips back to hers, her hair tucking back under her hat and books settling from the wobble of the cobblestones as she returns to the main road, hops back on her bike and cycles backwards out of the frame while he un-lights his cigarette, taking it from his mouth, watching for her, and slides it back in the pack with the lighter in his pocket, and turns to look towards my window, checking in the reflection as he un-tightens his tie and instead of his face, sees mine and the world stops and he tells me that the opposite of love is not hate, it's indifference and I climb out the window and he gives me the cigarette pack of Woodbines, which I throw in the window to you, flip the frame back and he and I entwine like vines of woodbine and honeysuckle in a midsummer night's dream.

Rhythm and Blues
Lauren Voeltz

Drivin' my deadbeat, rust-bucket blue Malibu into the hotel's parking lot, I half-think the police are gonna peep, creep up behind me, demand my ID, and tell me:

Move on. This ain't no place for you. Just go back to where ya came from. But the po-po are a no show.

I slide my slippery palms down my favorite corduroy jeans groanin', long and harsh. I'm prayin' you won't hate me, Daddy. I'm your girl, supposedly; seventeen, and alone in the world now, 'cept for you, I guess. What if you don't like me?

This Hilton Hotel ain't no place for blue-collar folk – like me and Ma. Collars probably need to be a pearly white, crisp and fine, to stay here. Will you have a place for me? I light a smoke, takin' long drags 'till my hands stop their shakin'.

I gotta get outta this seat. Get through those doors. I feel my nervousness itchin' under my skin. I called you a week ago, drove here to meet you. I know you're waitin' to find out if you jive with me or if we clash. I hope I'm good enough for you.

The car door creaks, grates as I open it. It latches when I slam it shut on the third try. I approach them fancy slidin' doors, not sure if I should feel gloom or glee. Now, here you are in the doorway. You don't look like me, 'cept the gray eyes.

You open your arms, and I stutter-step, shift, sidle into them. Your shirt smells like a laundromat. Your arms feel like Ma's... when I was young and scared. And my heartbeat – the rhythm – feels like singin' on Sunday mornin'.

What the Hell Was Your Mother Thinking When
S A Greene

she said never let him see you going to the toilet? she said always pay close attention to what he's saying as if you still find him interesting, and never bore him with your little job (excuse me? archaeologist?)? she said always take his side, no matter what a twat (my words, not hers) he's making of himself?

she said all men drink – even your father – don't make an issue of it? make him a Martini when he gets home (so we really *are* in the nineteen-fifties now?) a glass of wine with supper and a whiskey afterwards so he won't *need* to hoard vodka? she said always look cheerful no matter how miserable you're feeling? she said fuck him at least twice a week (at least she had the grace to blush when she said 'fuck') more if he's really highly sexed, and then he won't *need* to look elsewhere?

she said all men look at porn? she said all men get boorish when they're drunk and when you said I don't remember Dad being boorish she compressed her lips into a long-suffering hyphen that led to all the dark things she could tell me if she were minded? she said all men stray sometimes and it's best to turn a blind eye?

she said you always bruised easily as a kid, she recalls, and isn't it butter that's supposed to be good for bruises? she said well of course there's no excuse for hitting a woman but at least try not to provoke him and best not come round for Sunday dinner till your face heals because Dad would be upset? she said you don't just give up on a marriage and anyway didn't he apologise profusely and swear he'd never do it again?

What the hell was your mother thinking when she said don't be silly you can't move back with us! we're downsizing, anyway? And what the absolute fuck when she said what about all that equality business you're always lecturing me about? – next time grab *his* hair and slam *his* face into the door?

Bin Day
Philip Charter

The fitness freak at 34 performs lunges on the lawn. You wheel his bin towards the truck. Flip the top, and inside there's a pair of running shoes – running shoes you never use. When you look, your feet are bare. The supervisor taps his watch. Who knew rubbish was such a high-pressure game? The neighbour lunges. Left, right, left. The truck hisses. Day-glo men scurry. Bins jar and jolt. Press the button and in it goes, never to return.

The shop-window couple at 47A stifles a laugh at your outfit. Their condescending look smells worse than the truck. Your scratched-up seven-carat ring rattles the bottom of their bin. When you try to reach in, your arms have shrunk, and the harder you strain, the farther away it gets.

The lady at 74 puts her hands on her hips. 'Excuse me, Binman.' Her voice is a perfect composite of all the women you've ever disappointed.

'...We're called refuse collection agents now.'

'Do you take paper?' She opens the lid, and a series of photo prints flutter out. Into the air go ultrasound scans, away-day team shots, and thinning family portraits. The wind whips the cellulose reel all the way to the truck. She laughs. *'Refuse collection agent.'*

The supervisor taps his supervisor watch and marks his supervisor sheet. The lunger lunges. Curtains twitch. The lady laughs. Why don't you save them all the bother and just dump yourself? The compaction press reaches the top of its range. Three hundred tonnes of pressure ready to drop. You've withstood more.

As the mechanism starts its journey down, you set off towards the void. Gravel rakes your feet. Each pace faster. Air rushes past. Hole shrinking. Eyes screw shut. Smell intensifies. You only get one shot to break the threshold of a black hole. Build to a sprint. Leap...

Impact.

You're in.

Breathe.

Bed down among your smashed possessions.

Brace against the pressure.

But it doesn't come. When you open your eyes, the space of the loading bay extends forever. It's infinite. And the outside world now cowers in fear at the prospect of the inevitable crush.

Sea Monster
Caitlin Monshall

When we came to shore, we said we found her washed up in the cove, which I suppose was half true, and that we didn't know how she died, which was a lie. But no one seemed to care much about that part; they were more interested in her scales shining silver in the sunlight and, later, in the camera flash when the papers came and paid us for an interview. The museum took her and displayed her in a big jar of alcohol, and our names appeared on a brass plaque that read 'discovered by'. Scientists, tourists, garden-variety gawkers, they all came to look, though the liquid shrivelled her webbed, clawed fingers and turned her white hair brittle and translucent. The others went, too, but I never did. I saw her often enough; a thousand times as I hauled in the nets, writhing fish gleaming like silver coins under the decklight, with the sting of saltwater in my mouth and in the four deep scratches on my arm that never seemed to heal quite right. I saw her at the shore, in my sleep, on the sand, while the gulls wheeled and screeched overhead, loud enough to cover our footsteps but not to drown out her singing in my ears as I led the others to our usual meeting spot and pointed her out, gleaming like a goddess in the sun.

Chasing the Sun
Sarah Hina

There is a cathedral I return to.

Not the slim province of angels and resurrections, where long-lashed girls bow their heads in time to the dots and dashes of scripture. I'm talking about the long nave of recollection, where you and I spent a haloed youth wandering, and briefly touching, with fevers of words for trails, your brown hand my constant guide. Where a loamy scent led us past dead leaves and deader logs, into the quiet fix of the forest – the sacred altar. You touched my hair there, once.

This promise of the mind I retain like a yellowing photograph, smudged about its edges. Chewed on by time's chemical mouth, yet preserved in this tinny memory, this near-to-bled darkness.

Yet now you come. The stained-glass unloosening, shards re-assembling. You told me on the phone that marriage is a dead-end, the final purgatory to sense and sensibility. Your wife believes in miracles. You only believed in me, you said, and laughed to cover. You were never embarrassed, before.

I would like to believe in you. I would like for you to touch my hair again. But faith is a frothy, youthful affair, and you are as elusive to me now as that white god they sing to on Sundays. I love that old photograph, you see. I love pressing its terrible stillness against my tired heart. I cannot risk its loss. You will not see me at the train station tomorrow.

Darling M., my hair is gone gray.

Zap! Zoom!
Alexis Wolfe

I wish I'd photographed more butterflies. Those colourful ones, Red Admirals and Brimstones. Birds. Even insects.

Bees are long gone, ditto flowers.

I've even flogged the camera.

Everyone's on the move. Theories abound on the best places to head for, but no one knows for sure. Who can say elsewhere would smell less putrid than our street, with its eight weeks' uncollected garbage, its abandoned theme-park views.

No rash moves, not with Mum's medications.

Boom! she shouts from the bedroom. She's taken to only using calamity-speech.

I line up the four pills: a little blue circle, the red oval capsule, two tiny white ellipsoids, then crush them between two teaspoons. I rinse yesterday's syringe and fill a glass with cloudy rainwater. She lays motionless whilst I flush the pharmaceuticals down the feeding tube dangling from her floral pyjamas. The once translucent tube is now opaque and yellowing.

Some days I fantasise about going on the run. Nostalgia taunts me with memories of long-gone respite care, days I'd wasted window-shopping in town.

I keep an eye out for the postman. He covers the whole county now, so only comes monthly. My only source of cigarettes. Our shared fag butts are forming an orange mountain in the plant pot on the front step.

Sometimes I think about him whisking me away from my endless circular days of tubes and tablets into the world of his angular red post-van, crammed with rectangles and squares, parcels and letters.

Maybe I'm developing a crush on him. Or perhaps I'm just keeping him sweet because Mum won't last forever, and eventually—

Vroom! Kaboom!

—I might need his directions for the best way out of here.

After hoisting Mum window-side, I brew my coffee. Maybe we'll fashion wings from mailbags, soar like the birds we used to see.

Mum sits mannequin-frozen, eyes on the street, mouth the only thing moving.

Pow! Bam!

Watching intently for butterflies or superheroes who never fly past.

This Is My Hill
Paul M Clark

Aching back, legs, hips. It doesn't get any easier. Like climbing a mini-Everest these days. Shopping bags feel like breezeblocks with those handles that carve into your hand and make your fingers turn purple. Makes me growl and curse. But this is my hill.

Try a retirement village, my kids told me. I know they mean well. But this is my hill.

Grow old gracefully, one of the neighbours said. But there's nowt graceful about getting up to piss five times a night. And how's playing bingo with a load of corpses going to make me feel graceful? It's a slippery slope, I tell you. Next they'll be trying to get me to church. Get me closer to God before, well, I get closer to God. Fat chance of that!

I can see them over the road. Teenagers laughing when I mumble under my breath.

But they know nowt. Every step of mine up this hill is a separate smile. Because this is my hill.

See, I flew down here on my first bike, plastic wheels just-in-so coping with the cracks in the pavement. Then my Chopper as a teenager. I was bloody quick. Quick enough to impress Kara. We shared our first kiss at the bottom between the parked cars. On our wedding day, I carried her to our little house at the top and over the threshold. She were like a doll in my arms, light as a crisp. Heaved my kids up and down in prams while she rested. Watched her in tears, running down that hill for a longer goodbye, when our kids left home, one by one. Carried her down in a box when she left me. Holding back, because the only person I could ever cry with was gone. This is my hill.

And now I share it. Callum's like his dad, and his dad's like me. We all liked our bikes. Running's his thing, and when I watch him, it takes me back. He's a good lad.

'Need help getting up the hill, grandad?' asks Callum, racing past.

'Fuck off!' I shout. Got to keep up appearances.

The Four Simple Reasons Why I Used to Wish Bob Ross Was My Dad

Rachel O'Cleary

1. Because he would never shout at you. Ever. Mama told me once, after she'd picked me up from school, while we were eating grilled cheese and watching him paint a snowy landscape on the tiny TV in the kitchen, that before Bob Ross was famous, he used to be a drill sergeant. For twenty years, all he did was roar. He bawled out the men, made them scrub toilets, tidy their beds, and do thousands of push-ups. They all hated him. And then one day, he quit the army and vowed never to scream at anyone ever again. 'So,' she told me, 'anyone can change, at any time. Only, they have to really want it.'

2. Because you would never lie awake, clutching the edge of your blanket and startling at every moving shadow, if Bob Ross was your dad. You wouldn't be waiting for him to come home, wondering what mood he'd be in, or who might be with him. He would be right there, sitting in your bed. You would rest your face against the warm patch of chest peeking out between blue shirt buttons and feel the rumbling beneath your cheek as he read your favourite bedtime stories. And you would be asleep before you knew it.

3. Because Bob Ross wouldn't get angry if Mama burned the dinner, or spank Benny for making that ice skating rink on the front walk, or call you 'Girl Genius' for two weeks after you got a bad grade on your report card. He would just shrug and say in that duvet-soft voice of his: 'There are no mistakes, only happy little accidents.'

4. Because Bob Ross was always bringing home injured baby birds and feeding them patiently from an eyedropper, or letting a squirrel named Peapod live in his shirt pocket. And he would cup those tiny creatures in his paint-spattered hand and stroke them so gently with just the edge of his pinky finger, that it was like a solemn promise never to hurt a single delicate bone in their bodies.

Shadows Move Under the Old Skybridge
Jac Jenkins

We stand under the old skybridge in the weedful alley and look down to the vanishing point. The pavement is littered with debris, and on either side, windowpanes hang like guillotines. Behind them, the blackened air shivers, and another sliver falls with a plink. We used to come here for fun, for the hot tingle of fear, the carnal aftermath.

Standing here now, I remember extolling the Rubble Women, who selflessly cleared the streets of post-war Berlin, sorting out bricks for re-use. You laughed, declaring me gullible, and pointed out it was a convenient myth. Beside me, a sepia woman breaks the handle of her pick, thrusts the shaft into the hard ground and fades.

The shadow of the old skybridge tightens on us. You say something I can't hear, but I see sound coming out of your mouth in waves, each word in its own orbit, bobbing up and down. *Promised* jostles with *you* in a peculiar jig, as they always have – I want to untether them. Black air shivers. – plink –

I think I always knew about vanishing points. Parallel lines don't converge. The walls, with their shivering windows, stay a street-width apart. A skybridge spans the gap and eventually crumbles. I pull the shaft from the ground.

Burlingame
Mary Anne Perez

He thumped his thick fingers on the small screen in front of her middle seat, where their tickets landed them next to each other, and he tried to make the TV turn on because he noticed she had tried and given up, so he thumped again and she asked if that usually works for him and he chuckled and gave up his valiant effort so he could talk to this woman who he had noticed at the turnstile where she panicked to find her ticket and her pre-teen son jumped over, making her panic even more, and then when they were standing at the elevator he asked if she was OK and she shrunk a little because she wasn't used to being noticed anymore and her heart was still racing from the misplaced ticket and here they were sitting next to each other as she gathered her breath and told him they were finishing up a touristy vacation of San Francisco that week, taking in Chinatown, Pier 39 and of course the Golden Gate Bridge, and he was heading to Long Beach just for the weekend to see a 311 concert with friends and she felt the voltage of his gray eyes but the flight was only an hour and she already felt trapped in her seat because something reminded her of the frat boys who howled as she walked past their row of houses trying to get from the parking lot to class and she rose to the aisle as he leaned in and said he moved back home for his mother after his father died and that he's in Long Beach frequently because he loves it here and then asked barely audibly if she wanted to get breakfast but her ears were ringing too loudly to hear him and it ended on the tarmac as he finally pulled his duffel bag over his shoulders and walked toward the terminal and she noticed for the first time that he was tall and that his sandy brown hair softly touched the back of his collar and that all she knew about him was the name of his hometown.

Person Money
Zaqary Fekete

In my dream I was reading Banksy. He wrote, *'Your mind is working at its best when you are stressed.'*

There was a distant bang, and I woke up. I immediately coughed two very deep coughs, and then I held my breath until it went away. Yesterday the third cough had left blood on my hand.

After the bang, there was a series of footsteps echoing in the hall outside the metal cell door. For the past week, I had received food through a small window in the door. Yesterday there had been only one bread roll.

I could feel that this metal cell wasn't on the cruise ship. My last full meal had been on the ship where I had been reading Banksy's book of stencils. I remember the irony that I saw one of his prints graffiti-painted on the side of the ship the day I had boarded – the one with the girl and the balloon. That was one week ago.

Today no food came through the door. Instead, a piece of paper folded twice upon itself slid through. Then, after a brief pocket-searching scratching sound outside the door, there was a pen sliding after the paper. I grabbed the paper. It was blank.

After the hooded people boarded the cruise ship last week, they shot all the staff workers. The waiter who had brought me my meal was shot while he turned to run. My head was struck hard from behind. I woke up here.

As I stared at the blank sheet of paper, I suddenly coughed very deeply, and some blood sprayed on the paper. I sat for a moment and felt very bad. And then a laminated card slid through the door. I grabbed it and read it. The English on it seemed like it was software-translated:

'Sir or madam. We have no result of person money. If we are not re-sult by soon then there is the personal damage. Do you know valuable people? Today is the writing time for you.'

I read the card two times slowly. The card felt greasy and used. I dropped the card and reached for the paper. I started to write.

Banksy, how did you know?

Ice Cubes
Kerry Langan

He sits on his bed, the Latin book on his bent knees. Memorization is easy; he knows how to repeat something until it is so locked inside of him, it is him. Down the hall, his mother, also sitting on a bed, raises and lowers a glass of vodka to and from her mouth. The ice cubes dance to their own music, *tingle-tingle-tingle*, as they jostle in the colorless liquid. In other houses, this might be a pleasant sound.

'*Mater, matris, matri, matrem, matre.*' If he recites the declension ten times in a row, the ice cubes will stop tingling. He closes his eyes and softly says each word fully before going on to the next. When he finishes, the ice cubes chime with smug victory. He covers his ears and feels the thrush of blood in his head. He will decline a verb fifteen, no, twenty times. Twenty will do it. *Amo, amas, amat, amamas, amatis, amant.* He finishes the last recitation breathlessly and waits. Silence. His pulse jumps with hope, but the glassy melody of the ice cubes resumes, and he is already flipping pages. The verb, to hate: *Odio, odis, odit, odimus, oditis, odiunt.* A sliver of him, thin as a shaving of ice, knows that reciting something, anything, once or one hundred times changes nothing. But he can't stop. He starts to whisper the words, a hushed recitation. The ice cubes are noisy, but he is so quiet, it's as if he has melted.

Care
Megan Anderson

She leaves him in the barber's chair; time enough for one errand. When she goes back for him, he's bald. Every silver-white curl is gone.

The barber drops his eyes. *It's what he asked for.* A nod from the milky pink bonce. In sixty years, she's never seen it, but she can hear the words – *Take the lot!* – as if she'd been there. Part mischief, part cry in the dark. He's been asking for a new head.

At home, he is slack-jawed at the mystery in the mirror. He tugs his woolly hat low. He will reach for it before breakfast – before underwear – for weeks to come, an armour against conspirators and this new cold.

There are dragons outside. They've got clippers. They've been on the Big Dipper, but now they're on the travellator, heading this way. Better not let them in. His eyebrows are high. She pulls a cheerful rug over his knees and tells him there are no dragons outside. She tells him he's loved and he's safe and he's home.

I'm looking for the moon, he says. *You want me to swallow that orange?* It's a kind of a conversation, she supposes. Not like the old ones that went on for hours in front of the Aga, the pair of them taking small curios and turning them this way and that, back when they were bottomless.

Alaska comes on the telly, and she says *Remember the Northern Lights?* He is sunken jowls and glassy eyes. She returns to her crossword. Italy slid off her radar years ago. *Remember the years of living courageously? All those budgets on the back of napkins? Your affair? That wild moment behind the trellis? Our firstborn?*

None of it.

She's lonely and leaking time. His hair turns to bristle. She buys the paper for the death notices; she's not in there. She packs a bag (his woolly hat is in it) and swallows guilt like river stones.

He wonders where he is, asks about the gunman down the hall. Someone tells him there's no gunman. Someone tells him he's loved and he's safe.

Specimen 21: Primrose
Maia Rocklin

It's Earth, but she doesn't know that.

Through the viewport, many miles below, continents are defined by cobwebby sprawls of light and the black absences in between. The sun's slow advance limns the sea in gold, caressing the edges of a vast bone-grey pinwheel of cloud. Were she down there now, she would taste the promise of rain in the air, would know to seek shelter beneath the thick waxy leaves of a rubber tree.

But here, except for the drone of her life support systems, the whir and slosh of the waste disposal unit fettered around the lower half of her body, her senses are without stimulation. The capsule offers no scents for her to decipher, no breath of wind or rustle of beetle wings, nothing of substance to occupy her mind – only the bewildering images flashing before her eyes. Of a planet, and on it land, and somewhere on that land, a lovely green place bursting and squirming and humming with life. She can't recognize any of it by sight alone, yet she longs for familiarity, to move freely, to hear a heartbeat not her own, to touch fur or flesh or the smooth dappled skin of a ripe papaya. Even the cold sterility of her laboratory cage might be preferable to this torturous place.

She doesn't know they never meant for her to return.

Somewhere over the Caribbean, the oxygen generator fails, plunging her into a devastatingly complete silence. Her breaths grow rapid and then shallow, and for the first time in many long hours, she feels blessed gravity weighing down her eyelids.

And the stillness thereafter returns her to the jungle, to those inscrutable, muted moments when even the insects cease their chirring, when the other monkeys nestled in the branches around her utter their last, soft hoots into the dusk-lit canopy, as if to say: *We are here. All is well.*

Earth to Earth
Nicola Ashbrook

Four

My mum's knees make bowls in the green kneeler as she leans into the flower bed. I squat beside her. I watch as she scoops out weeds like ice cream.

'Want to help?' she asks. I nod. She shows me which are weeds and which are flowers. I pull out weeds until I reach my hand out of sight and pull out a handful of slimy slug.

Eight

My mum sends me to pick peas at the bottom of the garden. My fingernail slices through the pod, and I nibble sweetness straight from its green bed.

Twenty-two

We stand in my own garden, surveying the concrete and weed jungle.

'So much potential,' she says. We buzz with anticipation to turn the soil, fill it with lush fauna.

Thirty

We take the little one to the garden centre, where his chubby fingers seek water, and we sneak peeks at the bedding plants.

Thirty-nine

She sits on the bench beside the door, the sun gently caressing her face. Me and the children snip where she tells us; pull up this, tie up that – do as she would if she could.

Forty

I take five-minute breaks from her bedside to wander into the garden. Lime and scarlet foliage caresses my aching soul, echoing with years of her.

I crouch to the soil and think I hear it call her.

Forty-five

I stand in my new garden. 'So much potential,' I say. I'm filled with anticipation to turn the soil, fill it with lush foliage. But I rattle with loss.

Fifty-two

I stand in my son's new garden – a verdant landscape he wants to concrete. I say nothing.

Sixty

I kneel to weed, and little knees appear beside me. I show her which are weeds and which are flowers.

'Is that an ice cream scoop?' she says.

'It's a trowel,' I smile.

Seventy-six

I lower myself to the green kneeler, rubbing at my hip. I dip my fingers into the soil, letting its memories run over my palms. It soothes me.

These days it calls to me too. 'Soon,' I tell it. 'Soon.'

They Might Dress Boys in Pink Nowadays, but It Doesn't Mean It Suits Them

Sally Curtis

When we met, you were wearing prawn-pink shorts, which told me you would bring hot water bottles when my period clawed at my guts and, if I said I was tired, you would kiss me goodnight and nothing more. They denounced the imbalance of women in the boardroom and argued that society didn't need more refuges but fewer bastards who make them a necessity.

You wore them unapologetically. 'Look at me,' they declared. 'See what an enlightened man I am. See how in touch I am.' You didn't say you were a feminist, but you were the first to say, 'I love you'.

And I believed these pink philosophies as your alpha mates, masquerading in four-ply knits of complimentary lemon and mint, offered good-guy empathy:

'Never mind, love, there'll be more promotions.'

'I know you can, sugar, but I'll get it.'

'I understand, sweetheart. It must be bloody inconvenient every month.'

But when you thought no one was looking, eyes rolled, and the school-boy punster congratulated himself, and in brash camaraderie, you swept aside the trendy margaritas leaving the pretty parasols drowning in sludgy ashtrays.

In reality, your prawn-pink shorts merely disguised your flaccid toxicity; the fetid stench, engrained in the fissures of the skin, can never really be washed away.

I could have worked with the usual truths, played the game, but as I kicked against the glass, you brazened it out until, ultimately, holding shattered shards, you let go my hand. When my wage packet exceeded yours, and I upgraded our flights to first class and was bold enough to choose a car with white leather seats, the threads of your phoney principles began to fray culminating in a fondant donation to the women's hostel. All icing. All for show.

That's why, before I dumped your crap at your mother's door, I dyed your shorts black. And now they match the rest of your clothes so you don't have to pretend.

Pink doesn't cut it. Blood is red. Sweetheart.

These Beautiful Scars of Mine
J C Du Bruyn

These scars of mine.

So harsh and angry on my skin. Whether it's a cut on my knee or a scrape on my chin. They are unpleasant for sure, but they tell a story. My story. Every single one unique, like a written language only I can understand.

Some scars are not visible to the eye. Those never fully heal. They linger. Waiting to be picked, plucked and pulled like a scab to bleed once more.

Others are small and barely show, but the ones I made myself are on exhibit. For reasons unknown to others, I was a canvas for a blade. As I played games of tic-tac-toe upon my arms and thighs, I met someone.

He too had scars, but with a healing kiss upon my temple and the promise to have and behold, I would eventually call him my soulmate.

Our daughter arrived as perfect as can be. With eyes as blue as the heavens above from where she came. Cheeks as soft as the pillow on which she dreams at night. A smile so pure and innocent and a soul free from harm.

She gave me the waves of the ocean and the stripes of a tiger around my waist. I am not afraid to show them as they come from a place of love. I wear them with pride like medals.

These beautiful scars of mine.

Baby Teeth
Molly Millar

He was such a happy baby until the night he became something else. I'd run out of nappies and couldn't bear to wake him, so I sped to the shops and, on the way back, stupidly bumped someone's car. I stood apologizing over and over in my dressing gown until they finally drove off. The whole time he was lying in his crib alone. On the way home, I had a sick feeling, like knowing you've broken a bone before you move it. I could hear him screaming from the hallway. His window was open like a set of jaws, but I slammed it shut without thinking twice. I only remembered much later, scouring my brain, trying to think what could have happened to make him the way he is.

Around the time he should've started talking, he got so quiet. I became one of those brainless women who babble to their toddlers in the post office queue, sure at any moment his face would crinkle into a smile, and he'd point at me and say *mama*. It took me a while to get nervous, juggling his toys with my change at the cafe and laughing *any day now* to the other mums. He's five now. He's going to eat up all the days I have left.

I could tell him anything, that I wish he was dead, but my words would only disappear into his silence like a stone that never hits the bottom. I barely speak at all now, and when I do my voice croaks like the undead. He won't say a word but sometimes he screams. At night I'll find him curled under his bed or at the back of his wardrobe like a cat. His baby teeth didn't fall out but were broken, clumped together with blood in a fist I had to force him to open.

I know it's my fault for not being there when it got into the house. Now he can't speak, but he screams, and at night I find him watching something that isn't there in the corner of his room. We both hear it laughing.

Tell Me About Your Sadness
Samantha Palmer

'Tell me about your sadness,' he says. He rolls a cold beer over his cheeks; they're red and scorched despite me slathering him in sun cream.

I laugh. 'What if I don't want to?'

'Come on.' He blinks at me with stubby eyelashes, leans back on the couch. 'It's boring if you don't play.'

'You think everything is boring.'

'True.' He rolls onto his side. 'Is it really bad?'

'What?'

'Your sadness.'

I shrug. My eyes slide over to the corner where my sadness is wedged, head forced down, chin touching chest. It groans to itself.

'Give me a dare instead.'

He smiles. 'I dare you to tell me about your sadness.'

'Not fair, you know what I meant.'

He passes the bottle. 'Life is unfair, get used to it. Have a drink.'

'I don't want one,' I say, but take a sip anyway. I like the bubbles.

Jake is not my boyfriend, but he'd like to be. I might like that too. I haven't decided. It's unspoken that time together is a test. We spend it exchanging barbs and trying each other on like vintage T-shirts.

'Mine is green and squishy,' he says.

I imagine it lurks on hospital wards; we've discussed his one ball and the ache of its ghostly twin.

'How big is it?'

He points from little finger to elbow.

'That's small for a sadness.'

'It's smaller than it was. Time does that, you see? Talking does the same thing. A problem shared is a problem halved.'

I don't want to say that a problem halved is still a problem – it's just broken with sharp edges. Besides, my sadness is not a problem. It's my glue.

I catch him looking at me. He's hoping his words are a knife that he can slip under my shell; he's a pearl hunter, and I'm an oyster. But I'm not sure I want him to see inside; it won't be white and shiny.

'I should go.' I kiss him on the forehead. I think I could love him. If I put the effort in. If I squint it into focus. 'Maybe one day.'

He nods. 'To be continued.'

Chronic
George Harrison

He wasn't well. He kept repeating himself, stumbling over syllables that turned to mulch beneath his tongue. 'They put little cows in boxes,' he was saying. 'The cows, baby cows. They can't move.' He spoke between sobs, sleep thick in his eyes and wet in his throat. 'It's like torture, and they do it because they can, for the taste. They're only babies.'

'Hey,' his mother said, taking him into her arms. 'Hey. Calm down. Breathe. What's the time?'

She looked to the display of the bedside clock in lieu of an answer. The latter digit shifted under her watch, blinking away and returning as something remade. And still he continued in his ramblings, holding forth with a demented fervour about the dream he had just woken from. 'I was in a box, with the cows. I tried to move, but I was trapped, and when I tried to stretch out, there was nowhere for me to move.' Even as he spoke, it seemed as if his tongue was expanding into his palate, fattening in preparation for the slaughter. When he was younger, he had woken her with other fears: for a while, nuclear wars and then, later, black holes, the concept of eternity enough to unsettle his precocious mind.

'It's okay, baby,' she said. 'It was just a dream.'

She stroked his hair and felt the evening of his breath against her. His shoulders shifted with each inhalation, and the crying slowed. Eventually the choking sobs were tamped down his throat, pushed back inside his body. He was still for long enough that the clock changed again, two digits this time, shifting in the red sinew of the digital display.

Then, 'It wasn't just a dream, though. It's never just that.'

He spoke quietly, beneath a lowering gauze of sleep. Before she could ask what he meant, the breaths sank into a deep regularity, and he was gone again. Back in his box.

Mother's Milk
Dutch Simmons

'Does it hurt much?'

It was like getting stung by a bee, a swarm of bees, over and over, angrily pricking at your skin, stingers darting in and out like tiny daggers until you no longer cared. Eventually you wanted the feeling to linger as you slid along the razor's edge of sadomasochism that is getting a tattoo.

'It's bearable.'

She stared with an intense mixture of loathing and curiosity at the images of patron saints that stood sentinel on my shoulder. One for myself; one for my son. A talisman intended to protect while projecting an air of spirituality intermingled with a reckless disdain for desecrating the temple that was supposed to have been my body.

'What if it looks weird?'

Hours prior, she made a spectacle of calling me 'a thug' for the never-before-seen ink that graced my living corpse. Racked with embarrassment and shame that she had failed me as a mother since I savagely rendered the very skin that once resided inside of her with pointless graffiti.

'You'll get used to it.'

Unless you live with your parents or swim together on vacation, there is little reason for them to see you nearly naked. Tattoos were hidden intimacies meant for myself and a significant other that no longer mattered, and yet my mother traced an acrylic nail the color of a ripe plum along the outline of my most recent addition and sighed.

'I don't think I could do it; the pain would be too much.'

She didn't grasp the irony of her own words. Having a 'nipple' tattooed would pale in relative comparison to the reconstruction surgery to rebuild her breasts from a double mastectomy. The tattoo would be liberating, addicting, pain would be rendered asunder.

'If you are so concerned about the pain, why bother with the reconstructive surgery?'

Her breasts, the same ones that nursed me to life and now, even in this moment of vulnerability, I wondered if the poison that resided deep inside her trickled over my tongue and down my throat through that sacred milk.

'Because I'm still a woman, and I'm not dead yet.'

Hyacinth Bean Rice
Vera Dong

I run to Grandpa's kitchen the moment I get up. Father is there, feeding the hungry, burning bellies of the twin mud stoves. Grandpa's back is bent, but his ladle, a conductor's baton. Alternating dark and translucent pork strips, waltz with purple hyacinth beans coated in shimmering lard.

In 1938, Grandpa brought one hyacinth plant with him when he and Grandma floated down to Nantong, a town two hundred kilometers further south, in a self-made sampan from his village stricken by famine and Japanese invasion.

'Grandpa, is it time to add rice?' I ask.

Grandpa nods.

I pick up a big bowl of washed rice, tilt it above the cast iron wok. Rice falls through my slender fingers, little by little, into the 'dancing duo'. Father scoops creamy pork bone soup – a broth bubbling through the night – and drizzles it onto the rice.

Since arriving here, Grandpa has grown hyacinth beans every spring. And every spring, he cooks the purple bean rice for neighbours.

At lunchtime, Father fills ten deep bowls; I deliver them to our ten neighbours.

Grandpa does not eat his own rice. He can no longer swallow.

Later, Father sits by Grandpa's bed. 'Dad, everyone said "Thank You",' he says as he steadies the needle. Grandpa tries to nod and smile. I watch from across the room. I can tell when the morphine has sunk in.

I hand Father my small silk hanky with a purple flower on it. He gives me a small bowl of bean rice with a purple sheen.

No More Plumb Bob
Pam Morrison

Alice likes to spreadeagle on the bed, arms and legs pointing like an ever-changing clock. It's been weeks since she shunted the bed legs off their precise east-west axis, which Ben, with compass, had insisted on. Those legs had screeched when she put her hip to the bed-end, shoving, grunting, inching the hulk off-centre across three wooden floorboards. Far enough to muck up the grid, she figured. To take back the whole shebang.

What pleasure to puff and primp the pillow, rumple the pale duvet inner, hauled out from its stifling cover. Then, like a poodle, to turn and turn, toppling off elbows and knees into any which way. Each time a fresh view: the pocked brass knob on the dresser drawer, the crack of light from the hallway; the whole cake of moon looking back at her through the square frame; the headboard where she and Ben once pressed their pillows flat, their untouched bodies in parallel.

He'd stood at the gate that day, plumb bob ready to plummet from his neatly bound right hand. Ben hated the lean on the left post. Alice twirled a tendril of hair and watched him from the kitchen window. Watched the heavy drop of lead swinging then circling into tightening eddies; kept on watching as Ben waited and waited, folding his impatience into cheek furrows, the crunch of jaw.

And then it stopped.

It was like a protest from the hot heart of the earth, Alice would think later on. That shiny point targeting the dead center, the black nylon cord stilling to an immaculate right angle: such perfect alignment could not be borne. Ben fell, and the plumb bob fell with him. Sucked by the earth or crushed by gravity, the Great Unknown had spoken. Or so it seemed to Alice.

Before the Water
Rachel Smith

She's here beside me, at our spot in the doorway of what was Video Ezy. You can still see the faded orange branding on the window, old returns piled up inside the glassed door. I'm counting time, all those seconds building up to now, fifty-seven hours and twenty-two minutes, the world shrunk down tight to the fishhook pull of my guts, and I can smell that fried chicken shop ten blocks away, the one I used to go to after Saturday night drinks with the boys, can feel the thick slip of noodles from my favourite Chinese place across town.

She stirs and leans on in, eyes half shut as she tells me about her dream, how she was trapped inside a small dark space, couldn't see it but could feel it like you can in dreams, and when the lights came on, it was wall-to-wall ice cream, that fancy gelato stuff they used to sell at the Viaduct before the water came up, and then the walls started to close in like an Indiana Jones movie, and she had to eat her way out, woke up with sugared fur on the back of her teeth.

And there it is, the tang of sweet on her breath, and I know then that the rustling last night wasn't rats like she'd said.

She looks up at me, all open eyes and mouth and exhale of day-before sugar, as if we're back at home, the two of us across the table like that last dinner before we left, her in a low-cut red top, our eyes on the plate of food between us, mashed potatoes and the crumbed schnitzel I'd swapped with the guy across the road for my out-of-date meds. She looks up at me as if this is how we'd always hoped it would be.

Fifty-seven hours and twenty-four minutes. I push my lips against hers, breathe in her wetness, bite her tongue. Taste its sweet sweet iron.

Terra
Anne Howkins

Terra /'ter-ə/ noun – earth or land

Terra firma, you said. Solid earth, stay on it.

Then, walking your three hundred acres, pride seeped from your bones, spilt onto fertile loam. Yours, no one else's. Our children's inheritance. Nothing beats owning land.

You called your feral grandchildren home at dusk, grass-stained, bramble juice sticky, scooping them up like emeralds and rubies, brushed golden stalks from their hair. Watched them sleep, heavy-limbed, piled like puppies on the floor. Contentment spilt from glowing windows, pulling your family irrevocably home.

Terrestrial /tə-'re-st(r)ē-əl/ adj – relating to land

Barley heaped in the grain store. Your liquid gold. Your annual victory against the bloody British weather that floods your fields, parches, floods again. The grandchildren's straw-bale dens and castles, fought over dawn till dusk.

Friday nights, the pub floor unwiped boot mud-slippery. Farmers propping up the bar, railing against the foreign muck the youngsters drink, brewed from barley grown in a country your grandad died fighting against, the youngsters not interested in tending the land.

Terrible /'ter-ə-bəl/ adj/adv – serious

When we call, you can only talk about the price of seed; your bank balance; the scarcity of seed; the constant record-beating deluges; re-seeding; the burning days, so hot the dogs yelp as their pads meet the farmyard; the newsreaders' unprecedented this and that; the heat; barley smut, seeding blight, leaf spot, blotch, rust, mildew; the cost of spraying; the half-full grain store; the earth worn down to dust; the quarter-full grain store; your overdraft.

You don't talk about the nights you take the twelve bore out of the locked cabinet. Hold it, undecided.

There is nothing we can do.

Terror /'ter-ər/ uncountable n – very great fear

Run, we say, leave the farm. Take yourselves, the dogs, anything portable. Just leave. Follow the feral cats, the deer we spied on at dawn, the badgers the children watched at dusk, the swallows and the swifts fly away from the land.

Fire licks at the hedges you refused to destroy, consumes whole fields in single gulps. The grain-store resists, yields. You think there is not enough water in the world to stop it.

Our phones ring.

We can only hope.

Three Hitherto Undocumented Ghost Recordings
Barclay Rafferty

Whisky coaxes fisher-folk. Farmers prefer bitter.

Pubs are fertile hunting ground come last orders. Patrons'll pour their hearts out when their mouths are dressed. Some get possessive. *Sore throat, can't sing well*, etc. I don't mind, I tell them, tapping the red circle, tilting the microphone. Streaming services don't have everything: songs of local environments, passed on orally, altered, updated.

One customer smooths a Fair Isle pullover, claims the most beautiful song she ever heard was whistled one night from an open window. It comes back, now and then, in fitful dreams, and another thimble-full, she reckons, searching for the note, will bring it closer.

I doze, impaled by a beechwood chair, dream of Dad in thundery Glasgow. On waking, my spine's branded spindles. We sleepwalk, across peatland, catch movement from a lighted window. The latch clacks. We dither, anticipate Fair Isle's song.

'Have yous got no homes to go to?'

~

Lost, you repeat.

Another Sutcliffe lane. Your car sputters by a wall smudged green with moss. We rucksack past houses with postage-stamp windows, large chimneys, gables jutting up into slate-grey roofs. A builder's nightmare, you say. Wonky gutters on a steep hill, not a straight line in sight. But they work, I say. Better than accidentally camping off the A9, near Cairngorms, Aviemore, wherever.

Your right foot quicksands; the left hopscotches. 'Turn on the headlights, I've trod on a hedgehog, a hillock.' We drain battery: some bloke in camouflage, lips parted, nostrils flared, eyelid twitching. The stream cuts, a buffering circle, your running commentary.

The archer's quiver, his arrow true, the bow released.

~

Heard you became an events coordinator, mate, in Yorkshire, East or West Riding, definitely in that part of the country. Loads of folk clubs up there. Last time we spoke, you mentioned your thicker-than-waters being carted, single-file, down the old church-way, to the chapel of ease. Never thought we'd be that close again, hash and lipstick irises. Asked if you remembered your mum penguining down Coffin Path. How you told her to watch for overhanging branches.

How she turned, said you're just like Dad. That you're in your father's thoughts. That he says hello.

Quiver Pie
Nancy Freund

Melanie teeters into the dining room, her lurid red quiver pie wobbling on her great Aunt Mary's silver platter. No party, no picnic, no husband anymore; this is for her son, waiting at the table. She traded shifts to do it. About time. Today no singing for the Bloody Mary Breakfast Men in Golf Stud's Club. No teasing lipstick celery sticks, no Mimosas, no Bellinis. No women who check out her pencil skirt, her knees, her neckline when she rolls her chin and flips her hair. No tricks for tips today. Today is Ted's. He watches her approach.

Suspended clouds, pine nuts, cherry Jello, orange zest... she never reveals her recipes, but he's her kid. He knows. Her clouds are marshmallows, microwaved and molded. Pool-party people always ask, but she just smiles, lowered-lids, and tuts a finger like Aunt Mary did when asked her age.

Teddy's twelve, unimpressed by break-an-ankle heels. She wears them for herself. Melanie's an earthquake; she brings down the house, even entering a room. Men tremble just to watch her mouth work. Doesn't matter what she sings.

The gout-wren her prior husband plucked appeared to have a throat, all puffed up feathers, but she has no song at all. Melanie belts out the requests, stretches on her toes into the microphone, very 1940s. Perfect pitch. She sets down the plate and hands her boy a fork. She'll snap up another lover soon. And another. She'll sing them all to sleep. She sits.

Ted's father craved her sweet sounds and candy-blood desserts, and then he bolted. She sings Ted the song she wrote last night on her bedside notepad meant to capture dreams.

His mother's changed today. No birthday song, no candle, but Teddy blows his wish out loud. *Every breakfast, quiver pie.* He forks his tines through her clean red membrane, plunges deep and plucks a cloud. Gummy-suction. She sits and runs her pendant on her chain. She knows who she'll target first. Cowboy boots, big buckle. Ted pops the blob into his mouth. Swallows whole and holds her secret safe.

Postcard
Corin Burnside

A postcard came today.

On the back, she'd written one of her updates, signed it with a big swirly *A* and a smiley face.

My vision had blurred, and I'd wiped the heartache from her words, smudging the ink as I pinned it to the corkboard alongside the rest of her new life.

Let them go, and they'll always return – I read that in a magazine years ago. Against my instincts, I'd never held on too tightly, given her the freedom to go if she wanted. And when she did, I found myself waiting for an age, unable to move on with my own life, mourning what I thought I'd lost.

The policewoman touches my arm.

'Is there someone I can call?'

I'd forgotten she was there. Shake my head. Me and Amber, we're a team, there's no one else.

'If you're ready then.'

I lift my bag and follow her out of the house, which stopped being a home the day Amber left. The constable behind me closes the door.

The lights on the police car rotate as if they belong to a fairground ride, red and blue, brightening the dull day.

Curtains twitch along the street. Let them stare, I don't give a damn.

As we pass the park, I cast a final glance at the destruction we couldn't prevent. The place where she and her friends played as kids, swept away in the name of progress. Despite our efforts, we failed but knew we'd done the right thing. I'll plead guilty but never be sorry.

I only hope she understands why I did it.

A chirrup comes from my bag. The WPC nods at it.

'Get that, if you want.'

I fumble, nervous hands clumsy with the clasp.

It's Amber. She's sent a link; a report of the protest and a picture of me, swinging off the front of a JCB, spray painting the windscreen.

I look like a madwoman.

A message appears.

I'm so proud of you. X

At the traffic lights, a ray of sunlight breaks through the clouds and falls on my face.

Gaspard's Thoughts
David Bridel

The gurney rattles across the uneven floor. The exhausted faces of the orderlies.

Broken windows, fluorescents blinking. Muffled shouts behind doors.

Lurch! Over a huge crack between corridor and defunct elevator. Gaspard thinks:

In the end, I'm not worth much. Gaspard thinks:

I *was* important. People sought me out. I had opinions. I wrote to provoke. Gaspard thinks:

All the thoughts I've had in my life. Tens, hundreds of thousands. Crowding, crawling, jostling, bullying. I did their bidding. When I thought I was foolish, I abased myself. When I thought I was injured, I took revenge. When I thought I was strong, I chased my dreams. When I thought I was inadequate, I chased girls. That time I was late to meet you at the airport, I thought I was a terrible father, I called your mother and screamed at her, she's never spoken to me since. That time you gave me a watch for my birthday, I thought you were dismissing me, there was no engraving on it, I flew to Madrid on a whim, missed your wedding out of spite. The things that never happened that I've conjured in my mind, the losses, the humiliations... The things that *did* happen that I corrupted, the promotions (envy), the publications (luck), the gratitude (sneering). Worse: the thoughts that I was given, ceded, that I never bothered to examine – this is the truth, this is the gospel, this is how to live, this is a sin. No wonder, thinks Gaspard as the gurney races into the operating chamber, as he observes the vast, creeping crimson stain on the dirty grey sheet covering his stomach, no wonder the night sky screams with pain, no wonder the city trembles beneath the crushing impress, our very thoughts are at war; what I think is right, you think is evil, the wine we drink, the altars we build, the ideas we cling to... Invisible armies of righteous thoughts, hell-bent on destroying each other...

The nurse is haggard, handsome, he thinks. Oxygen smells like rose, he thinks.

I neither matter nor don't, he thinks. My son will remember me.

Thoughts the soil, actions the weeds—

A Ghost in Paris
Natalie Belousova

JB & KS, 2018, Toujours amoreaux, proclaims a padlock on the Pont des Arts. 'Forever in Love', but she doesn't know if the syntax is correct. Were they a French couple or an American couple using French to sound more romantic?

She thought her French was okay, not great, but enough to get by. But now she's here, the words and phrases she's spent months studying slip away like water through open fingers. She can only whisper *bonjour* or *désolée*. Even old faithful, *je ne parle pas français*, escapes her now, not that it isn't obvious. Sometimes people take pity and speak to her in English, but most don't bother. *Stupid tourist*, she imagines them thinking. She has no idea how that sounds in French.

Her debit card doesn't work here. She's relieved to find that at least the ATMs accept it, faithfully dispensing stacks of Euros, and so she's using cash everywhere, like she hasn't done for years, like nobody's done for years. She feels like she's disappearing, a ghost wandering the elegant streets, leaving no trace of her passing.

Her eyes fall on a woman sitting in a café, wearing a striped dress, cigarette in her teeth, and small dog in her lap. A living stereotype. She wants to take a photo, but she's too scared of being noticed. The dog senses her like dogs always sense ghosts, and it starts barking hysterically as she walks past. She hurries away, face burning. Behind her, she can hear the woman berating the dog, nonsensically: 'Dis pardon! Dis pardon!' – *Say sorry! Say sorry!*

She smiles at this, pleased that she understands at least this little phrase and amused by the pointlessness of it and the woman's unapologetic Frenchness. She takes out her phone, wants to text the story to her friend back home, but there's no Wi-Fi here, and she hasn't been able to get a SIM card.

Her smile fades. The French words for *I am lost* float up lazily from her memory and take up residence in her mind. '*Je suis perdue*,' the ghost whispers to nobody. '*Je suis perdue*.'

You Know This Is How It Is
Louella Lester

You're on a beach. Not a travel brochure beach. A real beach with a mix of brown sand and pebbles, and even stones. A few weeds and a strip of algae along the waterline. Perhaps a forgotten plastic pail.

The air is just above a shiver, the sun now only a slash along the horizon. But warm enough for your misshapen white T-shirt and ripped cutoffs. For flip-flops indented to fit only your feet. Maybe a thin cotton wrap around your shoulders.

You sit and breathe in. Not a perfumed air. Real air with a whiff of dead fishflies and forest fire smoke and the brackish pool of water nearby. A linger of dog poop or skunk. Perhaps your own leftover sweat.

The barbecue was good, as good as your family can be. A few hugs and laughs and snickers. Not the usual yelling or tears. Maybe worth repeating next year.

You run your tongue across your teeth. Not minty or flossed teeth. Real teeth harbouring hints of garlic and onion and cheap wine. A string of stuck celery or bits of corn. Perhaps the chemical bite of charcoal.

The stone is smooth, as smooth as the evening-calmed water. Thousands of years of washing and wearing and polishing. Then waiting here on this shore. Maybe touched by no one until now.

You send the stone flying out over the lake. Not a perfect stone. A real stone that skims and skips its way into the distance. Angling up or down. Tripping long or short. Landing clear or messy. Perhaps mimicking the phases of your life until it sinks like the sun, one way or another.

Sunday Service
Jessica Katherine Andrews

Every week after church, we count out our admission to another world.

Our hair blends together in the salt-sweet dark, and for one hour forty-five, we're anywhere else. My neighbour Ellen waits until the opening credits to slip sherbet lollies reverently from her sleeve, and we suck until our tongues bobble and split.

In this one-screen town, every movie becomes a prayer. We've seen this twice before: the boy loves the girl, but he doesn't know until one day she gets contact lenses and her best friend straightens her hair. Then, he's practically speaking in tongues. When they finally embrace, Ellen grabs my wrist urgently, and my heart swells like a popcorn kernel ready to ping.

After, we leap between streetlamp spotlights in the parking lot. I sweep my pink glasses off dramatically, and Ellen's bracelets jangle a psalm as she pretends to be struck gaga in love. The halo around her head tells me rain is near, but as our lips meet in a Big Screen kiss, none comes.

I know this isn't love because where are the thunderstorms and the makeovers and the milk-eyed boys? But after Ellen's mother pulls away in their grey Sedan, I'm suspended, swollen-tongued, until Sunday comes around again.

The Philatelist's Promise
Sharon Boyle

I'm on my back, knees bent and spread, my vagina exposed. The nurse asks me to relax. I stare at the ceiling of polystyrene squares and wait, mouth closed, mentally humming, not thinking about dodgy DNA.

'What is...?'

I crane my neck. 'Everything okay?'

The nurse *mmms*, removes something with a pair of tweezers and performs the smear test.

As I'm heading for the door, I see it: a postage stamp in the kidney-shaped bowl. First class.

The Queen's head on my vulva? What would Mother have said? She was a royalist – not the cavalier type, for she was, conversely, puritanical. She'd regularly clasp my hand and deliver the *treasure your dignity* chat when I succumbed to hormones.

I pass the loo in the corridor, remembering I'd whipped out a wet wipe from my handbag and given myself a quick clean for decency's sake. Should I be mortified or amused? A story to tell the girls or keep quiet in case a less than spotless muff is deemed unacceptable? Will it go on my medical record? Be the talk of the staff room? Will the nurse bin the stamp? Not use it, surely, no matter how hard-up the NHS is.

A letter arrives from the surgery. I study the first-class stamp. Mine? Positioned and pressed – return DNA to sender? I open the envelope. They want to see me – something about a colposcopy. My cells must be misbehaving. I think back to Mother, her mouth pursed, not telling us till it was too late. Weightless and white as if made of chalk, she lay on the hospice bed, full of condemned cells.

I scissor round the stamp and slip it into my purse – I've started collecting them, growing fond of the Queen's side-on look that dare not meet my eye. Just like another regal lady who squeezed my hand and whispered the *treasure every minute* chat in her final days. I didn't tell her I hadn't inherited her cavalier attitude to health warnings or that I grieved she didn't do battle. I just squeezed back and promised.

Mirna and Davor in Sarajevo 1995
Emma Phillips

The hardest part was staying put. When her mother beat dust from the blankets, Mirna felt pieces of her soul spill from the window and rise like butterflies they used to cup in their hands before the war. She remembered how their wings beat frantically against her palm in a bid to be free. These days, freedom was tenuous; no one except snipers ran in the hills, and Mirna only saw the landscape in pictures. She drew her memories in notebooks and hid them under her mattress so that her brother couldn't deface them with his rage.

Davor's anger spilled out with the dust. He beat the cushions with so much force that her mother asked if he could fill the gaps in the stuffing with his frustration and if not, perhaps he could help her tear Papa's shirts into pieces to give them more to lean on. Now, even paper was a commodity.

Mirna's drawings became smaller. She sketched tiny dragonflies around the edges of old letters, drew the hawks which still circled the hilltops at dusk and practised painting the flowers her mother loved to pick from her grandmother's garden until they were so realistic, she almost filled her empty vase.

Once, when Davor was grounded for taking the gun he'd found in Mr Ahmetovic's apartment, Mirna had drawn his portrait on the back of a poster she unfolded from his pocket. Davor was fast losing his boyish features, and Mirna searched his face for signs of the man he'd become. When he was sleeping, Davor wasn't angry. Then one day, after bringing the war to their apartment every day for months, he was gone. Mirna searched his room for clues, listened to the silence. On his mattress, Davor had left pencils.

Inheritance
Bwalya Mumba

'Sorry I'm late,' Gawa says, placing a cold Mosi bottle on Chewe's grave.

He unfolds a floral print chitenge, sets it on the ground, and sits beside his wife. Gawa bites open his own Mosi and fills his mouth with cold lager. Chewe's bottle drips condensation onto her black-gray tombstone.

Gawa drinks, distracting his thoughts and urgency; snaking his eyes over the cemetery's broken earth and bush flowers.

'There's this thing called love languages,' he says after emptying the bottle. 'I found out about it recently – thought it was stupid at first. But... there's something to it. I think 'touch' would've been your language.'

He opens another bottle. The beer bubbles, pops, and smells like a hangover.

'This is my last visit,' Gawa says. 'I hope...'

Talking to the marble beside him feels silly. He tries to imagine it's eight years ago; he could believe she was listening then.

'I tried, baby,' he says, 'I planted myself in the life we made as hard as I could. I kept our flat, our car, our friends – even Chanda.' She'd have laughed at that. 'I tried, but the years have rained on me and, I think, washed me away.'

Gawa's thumbs drum his second bottle.

'When I look back, I barely recognize the me that had you. And you... aren't here. You're not the bones in that grave or the bits of memory in my head. You're not here.'

He puts the bottle down and plucks his silver wedding ring out of his pocket. Gawa balances it between his thumb and index finger like a coin. The person he is cannot inherit it. His thumb flicks the ring into the air. It catches sunlight as it spins up then down, landing with a thud a few steps away.

'Bye,' Gawa says.

He rises from the chitenge and walks to the ring. His shadow swallows its silver sparkle as he stands over it and crouches down. Gawa palms the silver band into the ground and brushes loose dirt over it. He imagines someone finding it; he imagines it staying here forever. He gathers his things and leaves her beer.

Herr Friedrich's Fabulous Kabarett
Philip Charter

1925

At curtain up, Herr Friedrich drinks in the atmosphere. The splash of cymbal, pitter-patter laughs, the slivers of expectation that filter through tiny gaps in the crowd, the pause before the next act. Spotlights track his movement across the stage as he sprinkles his set with tonight's blend of risque comment. Ten years ago, this scene was unthinkable.

'Ladies and Gentleman of Berlin, I present to you the fabulous Günter and the Wolf.'

The room crackles in anticipation, and first-date couples break into Riesling-soaked smiles. When they see the wolf is a dachshund with a set of stick-on ears, they groan in contentment. Günter wears a dress. The act is a riot. It's fabulous, like all the performers in this fabulous kabarett – airborne acrobats, strong-thighed chorus kickers, and radio voices with movie-star looks.

The audience changes every night, but their laughter stays the same. Velvet red lips and the weight of the silken top hat. Bank notes flutter. Electric surge. Ash-stained floors. Rapturous applause.

1935

At lights out, Friedrich stares into black, hands clamped to ears. The rumble of trucks and the bark of orders squeeze through his fingers and into the swirl of his deep, dark thoughts. Strong light strafes the window. Residents await the next act.

'People of Prenzlauer Berg. We have papers for Friedrich Finkel. Direct us, or we will force open doors.' A nightmare ten years ago, reality today.

Jaws clamp shut, fingers on lips, legs swing out of bed, and the audience sits side-by-side on trembling mattresses, listening to the dread through mouldy, creaking walls. A candle flickers – the soldiers note the presence of a good citizen. Not all residents are canvas-hoarding artists, long-nosed sons of watchmakers, or academics with patched-up glasses.

The accusations change every night, but the outcome is the same. Machine-gun instructions puncture the sleep of this run-down boarding house. The pounding of tires on cobbles, the smack of soles on floorboards, the grand unveiling of the charge sheet, and the stifled sounds of prayers behind thin wood and rusted locks. Friedrich stands to face the music. Heart in mouth. Steps approach. Rap on the door. Silent applause.

Encore. Encore.

Balmedie
Claire Griffiths

It's the bones washing up on Balmedie Beach that sets the tongues to talking. 'Fishing twine,' they say. 'Black bin bag, bound tight. Nothing accidental about that.'

Jackdaws circle unseen winds, taken by the currents.

I see her now, at our battered table at the White Horse. We eat before she does the test, picking at a portion of grainy mac cheese. Unceremoniously, she grabs the *Dickies Pharmacy* bag, takes herself off. In the emptiness that follows, I see all endings.

She doesn't look for me as she exits the toilet. I catch her at the bus shelter, icicles glinting like teeth.

'Positive.'

The ride home's silent. She gets off at Millden, me Blackdog. My calls after that unanswered. I hear she runs in September: 'London,' the tongues say, 'or Cardiff.' 'Didn't even say goodbye to her Ma.'

Fifteen years pass; the North Sea releases. But fishing twine weakens. Bin bags shred. Bones dissolve in salt. No reason, then, for me to cast this line across time – to think of her (of it) at all.

Except for that one time I catch her again, the Easter before she leaves town. My second-hand Golf, bought with Christmas earnings, creeps towards Cordiner's woodworks. She's on the pavement, diagonal to the wind, T-shirt flush to body. A wee pouch, apple-firm, peeps over the waist of her jeans. I don't slow down.

There's a roundabout at the end of the street.

'London,' the tongues say. 'Twine. Bound tight.'

And still, the jackdaws circle.

After the Bath
Rose Rae

'Just watch, Mum,' you say.

We stand there together, your body still dripping, and we watch. The swirling water splits apart, and a snake of air needles downwards, twisting the bathroom lights above us into a lightspeed-jump blur.

The needle dances. Always moving. Like your knees, balanced precariously on your chair at mealtimes. Your body, throwing itself into the people around you in the playground with total disregard of personal space. Your feet, tapping against the concrete as you stand by the teacher, forbidden from running until you *learn not to push.*

There is repetition. The same loops and spins, like a sock in a sock, spun around your head over and over and over. The sock hitting my eye and making me shout, wounded; hurt, though my eye is fine. Your face, blinking, lips twitching, a pantomime of the sadness that you know is expected but which makes no sense to you.

'I like the sound,' you say.

And there is sound. Soft at first, an imperceptible sucking. Like you, chewing on your sleeve, or a cup, or the tail of a plastic dinosaur until it is feathered to authenticity by your molars. Then it is loud. A chuckle, a screech of irrepressible laughter at nothing at all.

I fight the urge to cup my hands into the water and capture this tiny vortex. Delicate, precious, wild. As if I could control a primal force of nature. There are times when I could weep for a child who would just get dry when he's told to. But if you were any different from your own, mismatched, patchwork self, how could I find the beauty in a plughole?

Three Hours and Seven Minutes
Rosaleen Lynch

You steal three hours and seven minutes and I ask for them back, standing in the doorway of your flat, with you looking at me as if you haven't expected to see me ever again, after your theft, asking, 'How do you know it's me?' and I tell you, 'I've an irrational fear of being roofied according to my mother, lucky I don't listen to her, so I have this app on my phone that I check in on when I'm out and if I don't, my phone starts recording to the cloud,' and you say, 'Oh', and I say, 'Yes, so you can understand why I want my three hours and seven minutes back,' and you look past me and ask, 'What do you want me to do, go to the police, what?' and I tell you I just want my three hours and seven minutes back, unless you want to give them to the police, but if not I could play the recording and this time I'd be conscious and make my own decisions or maybe this time maybe you could take the drug and I could take three hours and seven minutes from you, with consent and you choose option two and I sit in your living room, on the other end of the couch that I don't remember and watch a flicker of fear cross your face as your body slackens and your mind drifts, and I play the recording back; the bar, the taxi ride, the arrival at your flat, the assault, the phone for a taxi for me home and when the three hours and seven minutes are up, I leave and sometimes when I tell this story, you wake up before I go and say sorry, and other times you don't wake up at all.

The Weight of Things
Elodie Rose Barnes

Blue smoke. Blue sky. The day's news hollered from a kiosk. Train breath billowing. A guardsman whistles, slicing through her body like knives. Faded compartments, toe to toe with lunchtime's beer and her bag, precious cargo, nestled on her lap. The cake had sunk. It always did. Sagged in the middle under its own obscene weight. Too many plums, too much juice. Damp, bruise-like clouds drifting across a thick buttery moon, except it was margarine, not butter. Some form of alchemy. Four weeks' worth of paper-light ration coupons transformed into a greasy lump of gold.

Cigarette smoke. Glances raking over her hat, her dress, the third finger of her left hand. She'd kept the ring for men like this. Men whose eyes didn't see, who still saw it as solid and not a faint golden echo on her skin. A sunset. Outside, a body pushing itself along the platform, wheelchair flying, trouser legs hanging empty. Tattered peace banners flapping in the breeze.

The Voyage Out. The space between. New stops, new eyes, new curiosity. Her sister's birthday, explaining the bag, the cake, the special occasion that warranted plums and margarine. His watch ticking the train's rhythm against her wrist. The lightness of seconds, compared to the solidity of heartbeats. How long are you going to wear it, her sister will ask later, over cups of tea in the garden. Until things that seem solid stop turning to air, she'll reply. Now let's celebrate.

Another kind of alchemy, less welcome: the telegram, still in her pocket. Weighing on her heart more than paper ever should.

Grace in Camberwell
Jay Kelly

Swaying to a song I don't know, I see you, a perfectly familiar stranger, inspecting me. I am twenty and not unused to stares, but yours compels me, commands me, to retain this true and unswerving attention.

Performing for you then, I laugh with friends on the luminous, water-patterned dance floor, pretending my exuberance flows from them. I reach back and touch the floor with outstretched palm, then arc my spine forward almost a full three-sixty, just to unfurl for you again. Moments, or centuries, later, I return to my pint at the bar, swig cider luminous as red lemonade. My face is wet, my hair squally and dishevelled. You follow me, fingertips skimming the cotton ribs of my top. *I love your dancing.* I smile and examine your exposed clavicle for a moment before slipping away, back to the dance, as free as I have ever let myself be.

But later, I do not let you follow me into the bathroom stalls, only whisper instead, *I'm straight*. Later again, my head flat on the bar, you take both my hands in yours and plead with unnerving sincerity for just one date. I show no mercy, laugh you off and with it, myself; I was always so very afraid of reckonings.

Ten years later, I see you, single and solitary, walking Myatt's Field. I extend my hand, say *I'm sorry*, say *I don't know if you remember*. And glistering in that early May morning, you say only this, *Yes, I do. Yes.*

To Break a Broody Hen
Jo Withers
WINTER 2021 FIRST PLACE

We are new at keeping hens, you have a book, a 'complete guide'. You think everything in life can be read about and learnt.

One morning, the hen stays inside when we open the coop. She scratches and nips when we shepherd her out, growling like a terrier from her soft, feathered throat.

Hens become broody as spring approaches, you say, tracing dark lines across the open page. She is 'on heat', her hormones creating a powerful maternal surge. She believes the eggs hold her children, that if she sits long enough they'll hatch. She doesn't know they're empty, no more fertile than a stone. She scratches at the door again, scratches wild and hard so her feet start bleeding. You stare in wonder at her determination, and I remember how you dragged me from the hospital as all the nests around us trilled with life.

Your finger flicks to the next page, and your brow furrows. If we don't break her, she could die; she'll try day and night to reach the eggs. Her feathers will fall out, and she won't eat, she'll starve herself to death before she leaves them. I can tell from your face that you think this is unreasonable.

She starts to bang her head against the door. You unlatch the coop, and she runs in. Eggs are scattered in the straw, many wasted chances at new life.

You remove the eggs and place a cold, wet towel beneath her. You press her down, stroke her back, soothe her into submission. It's just hormones, you say – instincts urging her to nest. If we cool her down, it will subside, we'll trick her to accept her barren future.

I scratch a circle in the straw with my bare foot and crouch beside her. You try to make me stand, assure me that the cycle will be broken soon. I pull away, move closer to the hen, kneel down in the dust. We sit in silence, wait for our cold bodies to forget.

Oh, Look, the Stars Have Teeth

Jeanine Skowronski

WINTER 2021 SECOND PLACE

The morning that plane cracked in half, I thought mostly about poached robin eggs. A 737 down in a field, just two miles south of Banton College. You could see fire in the sky from our dorm room on the tenth floor.

Classes were canceled, so we went to the library. Sat on its steps for, I don't know, maybe, thirteen years. Bare calves against cold concrete. Nora left and returned with some lemons she stole from the dining hall. Harrah and I sucked on the wedges. Acid over oxide. We no longer smelt smoke.

Later-later, someone, probably Sharon Martin, was handing out candles on the quad, so we stood in a circle and lit them. The sorority girls cried; Nora laughed. I did what I had done all year; I stared at our feet.

Some night, maybe that one, Harrah invited the boys over to our suite. I poured Everclear into Hawaiian Punch. Nora made a playlist. Frank Zappa songs on a steady loop: 'Catholic Girls', 'Dancin' Fool', 'The Torture Never Stops'. Everyone got in a circle (again), but this one slowly widened. North and south pole magnets, pulled away from each other, toward opposite ends of the earth.

We were having a party, but no one was having a good time, so Harrah and I left, wandered off-campus and walked back and forth, back and forth, along RT. 229. Eventually, she laid down in the dirt and started making snow angels. And I laid down, too, because it felt like something we would do back in freshman year when we were wasted.

And it was nice, to stretch out and separate, to come apart, but pull back together, to scratch skin against dirt, at least until I realized I was looking up at the sky. At an uncanny valley that, for the first time, wasn't home to a sun that warmed me or a moon that guided me or a God that loved me, but instead, hundreds and hundreds of stars, made of hydrogen and helium and so many other things always primed to explode.

Ten Reasons Why I Didn't Stop Danny Jenkins from Throwing Your Brother into a Bin

Joshua Jones

WINTER 2021 THIRD PLACE

1. It all happened very quickly.
2. I thought someone else would stop Danny Jenkins. This was naïve of me. No one ever did. The nature of the bystander: an inability to take control or responsibility when part of a crowd.
3. I have an empathy score of 7/80. No, really. I didn't know this at the time – I was simply known as a *miserable git*. 'Dead inside', everyone said. I have come to learn that I have trouble processing my own emotions and identifying the emotional state of others in the moment. There's a great divide between my concept of emotion and my acknowledgement of it. Alexithymia – linked to my autism. I didn't 'feel' like your brother was in any distress.
4. Maybe my lack of empathy for his position, as the one being thrown in the bin and not the thrower, comes from a place of privilege. I have never been thrown into a bin, at school or otherwise. I couldn't empathise with your brother.
5. It was quite funny.*
6. Danny Jenkins was a brute. He was as happy slinging hooks as he was pushing people to buy chocolate bars out of his backpack.
7. Danny Jenkins sold me chocolate bars and energy drinks my mother didn't let me have at home.
8. One's silence is another's source of strength. I inadvertently gave Danny Jenkins the strength to throw your brother into a bin on school grounds. I wish I could say my silence was out of empathy for your brother, an offering of comfort, but it wasn't. This is more of an apology than a reason.
9. We were in Year 9. Your brother was in Year 8. This was the natural order of things – the food chain of the school years. Which is why, when you came to rescue your brother, we backed down. Even Danny Jenkins. You were a Year 10.
10. It was raining and I wanted to go home.

---

*What could I have done, anyway?

The Long Run
Claire Schön

1896

My sister watches from the sidelines, shrouded in grey, forced to wait.
    Sweat forms black pools dark as shadows. She matches you mile for mile, unrecognised.

1926

My sister leads the way, a violet streak, urging us on. You turn away.

1967

My sister passes the finish line, number intact. Light colours like her step; your bigotry bears no weight.

1972

My sisters join forces; you push them forward to keep them back, they won't comply. Feet firmly on the sticky black tarmac, waiting to run alongside.

1984

My sisters grow stronger. You keep their vibrance at length, but they are at your heels.

1990

My sisters have set the pace. They pass the baton; I continue what they began.
    Observing tradition: me in white, you in black, but we run side by side. The colours change, we reach a curve, decide to take it. A bump: I grow heavy, carrying our love around my middle, at my breasts and in my heart. We descend, hurtling, gravity improving your speed; I free fall. You race ahead, lungs full, your step determined. Your glory hangs golden in place of your heart. Our bands lose their shine.
    Fading to grey is not an option. I cannot return to the start; we must be seen.

Today

My daughter breaks the mould: she doesn't ask you but me. I'm not sure it's an honour; she's not to be given away. I give my blessing, my support.

I pass the baton.

She fires her own starting orders; she blazes in all the colours of the rainbow.

I wear my medal inside, in my heart, hidden, but for half the world to see.

Natural Selection
Mairi Smith

'Yah-god-damn-fidget!'

The blow, when it comes, barely registers, his ears still ringing from the sharp crack of his father's Mossberg Patriot. Eyes stinging, nose filled with the reek of cordite, Dwayne maintains his vigil of the distant tree line, but the wolf is gone, having melted away into the undergrowth along with the dying echoes of the shot.

'Pick the casing up, boy, and move,' his father growls, already on his feet, rifle shouldered.

A trail of snot and tears smear Dwayne's sleeve as he takes to his hands and knees to begin his new search, alert for the alien glint of brushed steel amid the moist carpet of pine needles and moss he'd been lying on. Ears clearer now, he's aware of snapping twigs and the soft brush of vegetation against cotton as his father, no longer interested in employing stealth, departs. But unlike before, Dwayne doesn't panic, doesn't care if he's lost, doesn't care if he's alone. Instead he welcomes it – the solitude – despite its transitory nature. For the blow won't be the end of it. A more comprehensive reckoning will be due, back at camp, by the fire, once the liquor begins to flow.

Dwayne draws in long breaths, shaky at first, then more even as he continues scanning the ground – patient, methodical – for he dares not return to camp without the casing. Bad enough that he'd jostled his father's arm; that might be explained away, a momentary lapse in concentration. Failure to observe a direct order could not.

Relief blooms when he curls cold fingers around the slim, cylindrical casing. He slips the spent cartridge into the top pocket of his hunting smock, buttoning it closed before patting it down. Rising to his feet, a small smile plays at his lips as he recalls the startled crouch of the wolf beneath the puff of earth that marked his father's wayward shot. Unconsciously his fingers caress the bulge of the cartridge as he pictures the wolf's stare – implacable, free, and alone – and he shivers with the sudden realisation of what he must now do.

Affair of the Heart
Jenny Woodhouse

Elsie opens the waxed paper. The heart plops into the pan, bouncing gently before it comes to rest. She adds carrots and onion. Joe likes braised heart: it reminds him of his youth, before he joined the Accrington Pals (old enough to know better!) and went off to the trenches. And it's off the ration. She doesn't mind cooking it for him, but she can't bear to touch it.

The water begins to bubble. She opens the door to the garden to let out the smell of boiling meat. Thank goodness it's summer.

He is out there as usual, his trilby flat on his head, prowling the lawn, seeking the enemy. He bobs down. Must have spied a dandelion. He'll be digging around it with his pen knife to free the root, pulling it up and adding it to a little heap on the path. He stands up, panting a little, and rubs his chest. Silly old man, she thinks, almost fondly.

Hissing and sizzling. The pan has boiled over. She rescues it, turns down the gas, and mops up the spill. The dishcloth is grey. Time to replace it.

She looks at the garden again. He's out of sight. She puts the kettle on, assembles teapot, milk jug, her coral-glass sugar basin, cups, saucers, apostle spoons. Two slices of the carrot cake she's made for Harry, who's due home from leave. Then she goes out to call him for tea. He doesn't like it to be late.

He's lying face down on the lawn, his hat beside him. His pink scalp is exposed to the sun, but it doesn't matter anymore. After she's called the ambulance, she turns off the gas and carries the pan into the larder. She'll have to leave a note for Harry. He can have the heart for his supper. Can't waste it.

Death-Chess in a Tupperware Box
Jake W Cullen

It isn't the first time I've helped bury something that is still alive. I brush the small mound of loam over the opening of your burrow, just after your tail disappears in the earth's darkness. *Goodbye.*

When I was young, I once trapped a wasp and a spider in a Tupperware box. I just wanted to witness the chaos. I hadn't anticipated that it would be a 72-hour game of chess, each life backed into its own corner. The spider spun a web over the three days; the wasp sat waiting. Eventually, the wasp bombed over. It stung the spider and simultaneously got caught in its web. As I remember, the spider curled up like the leaf of a mimosa in the rain, and the wasp writhed in the web – like you around our home.

It was funny to watch the wasp struggle for the next two days. On the final day before I buried it, it just seemed to give up. I used a crusty leaf to rip it from the web; its wings fluttered hopelessly like your lips before you cry. I got onto my knees and scratched at the mud, just an inch deep. The wasp on the crusty leaf beside its grave, the occasional spasm of a wing reaching out for help. I placed the leaf and the wasp in the hole and brushed the small mound of soil over them both. *Goodbye, friend.*

I read somewhere that wasps live for about 17 days on average, and according to the self-help book you were reading, the average human lives for 73 years. For the wasp then, 72-hour game of death-chess + 2 days of struggle + 1 giving up day = 25.76 human-years. I considered this as I helped to bury you, and it made our 2 chess-years + 1 struggle-year seem like nothing. I thought about the one-inch grave I'd given the wasp and the little fight it had left, and I thought about how you were insistent on digging the hole for yourself, as long as I helped to cover it, and I think about how far you're willing to dig. *Goodbye, you.*

She Is the Ball in the Pinball Machine
Nora Nadjarian

Her husband tells her *You are this, but not that. You should do this, but not that* and sometimes even *Are you trying to be something else, instead of this?* in monophonic replays. There are times when she scream-thinks *This is what I am now, take it or leave it.* It's her crazy-life as opposed to her goody-goody-life where she's ironing crinkles forever. Neon lights blink. Her lover presses the right button, and she's propelled and enters that flashing circuit until he pushes the left button, and the flipper flicks her like the *vescence* in effervescence, the walls zing, her whole body tingles, and for a nano-second, she rolls in and out of the mini question mark of doubt: yes, should I, yes? Another flipper catches her, and she's right in there now, in the giggly tunnel of all the good things, eye-popping admiration, tight-fitting love, fast-spinning lust, all of the above, and ping! She's going places, she's bouncing from wall to floor to ceiling, red turns green, pink zaps yellow, and she's laughing out loud, because *I'm this and not that,* because, for once, there's no why or because. There are ill-wishers watching her, they want to know, almost ask *What's a house-wife doing in this sleazy place and why does she look so happy, and who's that bloke young enough to be* – and she rushes past their gossip bubbles *Let them, let them gobble up their brain-cells.* A slingshot accelerates her course, and she never wants to walk a straight line, ever again, because *This is what I am when I'm with him, all this and more.* The next day is a real-life, straight-face day, and finally *Is this some kind of a joke?* asks her husband in his Yours Hatefully signature voice, and she says *No,* and it's the first time she's hurled a *No* at him, and she can see it going round and round inside his brain until it hits the target.

The Outhouse at Port Waikato
Emily Macdonald

Lorna is sleeping in the outhouse, a wooden lean-to addition to the fibrolite bach. Swaddled in sleeping bags and picnic rugs despite the sidelong sun, a big woman curled and semi-buried, incubating a painful decision – a revelation – I learn later on.

I persuade her to come out, insist even, saying the fresh air will do her good, and we step off the deck, cross the gravel track and onto the undulating black sand. The receding tide has left sodden trenches and uncertain ridges, and we scramble and slide, circling sink pools of slurry. In the far distance, the surf booms and retorts and sea spray hazes the horizon like smoke.

I talk too much. I try to tease out the problem, but with my eyes on my wet and sand-crusted feet, I bombard and needle, fencing her in with too many of the wrong questions. I ask about her move to Wellington, her work, and her social life. I ask about men – even though I suspect she has always preferred women.

If we had paused and looked up, if I'd let the wind slap some sense, maybe even if I had cleaned my sunglasses, it might have been different. The vast sky would have minimised, restoring proportion, and I might even have listened enough to hear what she needed to say.

Donut Holes
Sherry Morris

I was small, and you were tall when you said, 'Hey. Come here.'

I hesitated. You sat alone in the dim kitchen, at the head of a king-size table, clutching a bright-white box with a clear film lid. Inside were donuts. A delicacy in my house, a dozen glazed goodies stood at attention, under the command of your huge hands.

I came to you.

You often watched our grandkid games with a scowl and furrowed brow, your mouth turned down. Always held something in your shaking hands – a coffee mug in the morning, beer bottles in the afternoon. Evening time, long gulps from your whiskey cup distorted your face further. Mom said you were trying to fill the holes from some long-ago war. To play like mice. That deep-deep inside, without the drink, you were gentle, kind and nice.

You moved the box towards me. Opened it. 'Pick one.'

I inhaled. Smelled candy floss and Grandma's still-warm sugar cookies. My hand itched to take. Maybe Mom was right. I searched your face, wanting to be sure. Your John Deere cap hid your eyes. Maybe donut magic had sweetened your thundery mood and gravelly manner. Filled your inside holes with custard and jam.

You nodded once. A thrill ran through me twice. You picked me to share your special treat. Proof you were nice. Liked me, after all.

I touched the nearest donut, anticipated its fluffy sweet hit in my mouth. Stopped. I didn't want to seem too eager, too greedy, taking from the first row. I wanted to show grown-up self-control. That I was worthy of your precious gift. That I could fill the holes.

I tried a donut further back. It wouldn't budge. I grasped a third, denting another dainty cake. It stuck fast. When I tried again, you detonated.

'Stop touching them all. Take one!'

Reeling from your blast, I grabbed and ran outside. Crammed my mouth with donut, needing that sweet jolt. All I found was bitter hole.

The Half Life of Working Vocabularies
Jeff Gard

You lost a word just now as you wiped condensation from the mirror. Dripping wet from the shower, a towel draped around your goose-pimply flesh, you remembered the tall, narrow windows in Grandma's house, the one with a hideous iron grate in front of the fireplace, but on the mantel where you'd expect to see an ornamental, ivory cigar box, grandpa had mounted a flat-screen television. How out of place it seemed; There's a word for that – modern objects that invade history, a narrative element where eras collide like that movie with Heath Ledger, not the one he received the posthumous award for playing a psychopathic clown, but the one where he was a knight, and the jousting crowd chanted, 'We will rock you.' The missing word begins with an A; you chase it around your mind like a puppy trying to capture a butterfly. The word lingers, teasing and taunting you. Anthropomorphism? No, that describes objects that behave like people. Your skin cream comes to mind, the way the bottle has a bald head and knobby nose like Charlie Brown. And every time you press the top of the bottle, the almost-not-quite Charlie Brown sneezes a thick, peach-scented meringue into your hand, which makes you laugh like a child. And you still can't think of that A word, so you reach for your phone to look it up and think that no one had phones when you were a child. How did you learn anything? Contacting your friends was no easy feat. If you wanted to play *Ghost, Ghost in the Graveyard*, you'd ride your bike up and down the street – no helmets or kneepads back then – shouting at the top of your lungs until a half dozen dirty children appeared from nowhere. You still feel like that pre-teen on a bicycle, but when the mirror clears, you see the raisin you've become, lumpy and goose-pimply in your towel, holding the phone like some divining rod. You reach for your hairbrush, and the word appears: anachronistic. Relief flutters in your mind until another question materializes from the fog: How many other words have you lost?

But the Main Character Never Dies
Kate Armitage

She had always suspected she lived in a cartoon. The colours of her surroundings were too vivid for real life, with lurid hues of magenta and cyan. Noises came with onomatopoeic words encased in zig-zags for emphasis. It was enough to make her dizzy, to see stars above her head spinning in rotation.

Her parents told her she was being silly. She could tell they were tired of her complaints due to their visible emanata: lines and squiggles around their head that indicated exasperation. Or were they struggling to conceal the truth?

At the diner, she served creamed corn to a man-sized rooster and was pouring coffee for an alien as a regular customer arrived; a dog who stood upright and wore a suit. Every day he ordered a steak. When the local cat came in for a milkshake, the dog's eyes would pop out of his head, his mouth opening, long red tongue rolling down to the floor. The cat enjoyed this, drinking slowly through a straw whilst standing seductively, eyelashes fluttering. Then he would chase her out of the building. Every day it was the same. They would be back tomorrow. The steak, the milkshake, the chase.

Just before closing time, a six-foot chartreuse-coloured Praying Mantis came in. She asked him if he thought all of this was real or not. He said nothing, bubbles appearing out the top of his head, the final containing a question mark.

She was sick of her life being both banal and surreal. A waking nightmare. A bad trip.

When the diner was empty, she took the pistol from under the counter, placed it to her temple and pulled the trigger. But in lieu of a bullet came a flag from the gun's barrel with the word bang written upon it.

Independence Hall
Andrew Deathe

'...And over there,' says Justin, leaning down to his grandmother's wheelchair and pointing ahead, 'that's where they signed the Declaration of Independence.'

Maud lifts her hand to shield her eyes. He has faced her towards a road junction, and all she can see is the sun's glare on the windows of passing traffic. Where did they sign it? In a passing taxi? In a Wells Fargo truck? She isn't interested anyway. America has always been independent in her lifetime, what does it matter where they signed for it?

She wishes Justin would turn her chair so that she could get a better view of Jenny and the baby. Jenny is reading out loud an information panel about William Penn.

She's got the baby all wrong, thinks Maud. She picked it up wrong, held it wrong, and now she's got the poor child hanging in that harness thing that's going to do all kinds of wrong to it. It's not right strapping it up like that, facing away from its mother.

'So that she can see her way forward in the world,' Jenny had said.

'She needs to see your face, for reassurance,' Maud had tried to say, but her mouth refused to follow her thoughts.

If Justin would turn the chair around, Maud could see properly to correct Jenny. She drops her hands to twist the wheels and turn the chair herself, but there is nothing there to grip. The wheels on this borrowed chair are low, not like on her own. Her arms flail at its sides, a pointless doggy-paddle.

Justin sees her effort. 'You wanna go take a closer look, Grandma?' He pushes Maud towards the roadside, towards the Hall, away from Jenny, who is still reading aloud and unlistened to. The baby stares uncomprehendingly into the middle distance.

On a Rising Current
Dettra Rose

The piano arrived after Alfie's grandpa died, its walnut wood glowing like a firefly. It stood in the boxy third bedroom with noble pride, like a sacred site. Alfie hid his panda bear and Lego bricks in the cave below its lid.

Under his mother's tuition, Alfie's handspan strained to reach the keys. He had the gift; his mother was convinced of it. She played him concertos, ones she'd composed but never performed in gilded auditoriums. Alfie didn't know the word for longing then, but he understood it.

His face erupted in acne and bumfluff. He rolled spliffs on the piano and spilt cider on the keys and pedals. His mother locked the bedroom and hid the key. He knew the word sorry but never used it.

He slept on his mate's sofa and worked in a piano shop. After hours, he practised romantic classics, quietly. In the temperature-controlled Piano Bar, he wore a crisp dark suit and met Georgina, who shook cocktails behind the smoked glassy bar. She left jasmine on his collar and became his wife.

In their flat, magazines cluttered the piano. At night, Alfie composed. Melodies murmured in his bones. He performed for owls and cats. Nocturnal others, alone. He felt the wreckage of his late mother's longing and the aching of his own.

Sippy cups left sticky marks on the piano. His kids hid behind it. When their feet reached the pedals, he taught his twin daughters to play 'Chopsticks' – their chubby hands reminded him of starfish.

During their divorce, Georgina fought for the piano even though she couldn't play a note.

The piano hogged the lift – up it went to Alfie's high-rise flat. His new neighbour was the sky. Lifting the lid, he found wings of long-gone insects on the keys. He studied their patterns – transparent and brilliant. An intricate maze of curves like a fingerprint. How on earth did they get in there?

Alfie took a deep breath to blow them away, then stopped. Eyes closed, he pressed down gently on the dusty wings. Under his fingers, the notes took flight, fluttering upwards towards the disc of the sun.

Omne Vivum Ex Ovo
Sherri Turner

She cracks the egg into a small glass bowl, deft, one-handed. It slithers down and rests at the bottom, unbroken and flawless. She uses her mother's old whisk to smash the yolk and whips fiercely, the tendons on her forearm forming fine, tense ridges. The pale yellow froth no longer resembles an egg. Not a viable egg anyway. Not an egg that could grow into anything.

If she listens hard, she can hear the tiny bubbles bursting – pop pop pop. She tilts her ear to the bowl and waits for the sound to stop. Butter is dropped in a pan to sizzle until almost brown. She adds the egg, stirring, scraping. She uses her mother's wooden spoon, the one they used to make cakes with, the one she had been saving for when it was her turn. The toast jerks up with a startling ping, jolts her back to the almost burnt egg. More butter.

Coffee has been made, hot and strong, and its scent wafts up the stairs, calling him to her. She chooses his second-favourite mug, the one with cats on it. Today is not a day for favourite mugs. He enters the kitchen, pauses, watches the motion of her shoulders as she works. The stirring is the giveaway. No proud yellow yolk, sunny side up. No perfect translucent oval. It is the breakfast of failure. He slumps down on the barstool.

She gives him the moment he needs to hide his disappointment then serves him the broken egg on the hot buttered toast with a smile that doesn't quite make it.

He drinks his coffee, saves the hug for when it can be borne, thinks about cats.

Dear Jimmy Choo
Nora Nadjarian

Years after my wallflower adolescence, I sold my soul to you, you shoe-devil! On the night of the break-up (it was Christmas Eve), I was wearing heels designed by you and was teetering on fa-la-la and yet, miraculously, did not trip once. Mr Not-So-Right took one look at my Red Crystal Covered Pointy Toe Pumps and said how pretty blah blah, and I doubt he gave a blah whether they were made of glass, or gold, or wood. (*Step into these shoes, and you'll be a different woman*, the salesgirl had told me). As I gracefully excused myself and said I had to go and powder my nose, I hoped his heart would fast-forward to a near attack. I couldn't care less that my skirt climbed up and got mini-er as I stood up and walked out of the restaurant. The miles of corridor at the reception ended with a mirror and there were so many of me, one after the other, after the other. I admit I'd had one too many but, surely, I hadn't imagined his *I'm not really looking for a serious* – Had he actually said the R-word? I held my head high, even though my nerves were all frazzled, and didn't – couldn't – turn left or right, for fear of making my stomach tumble. But oh, the shoes I'd spent hundreds of pre-Xmas days saving for did me proud, so killer-stylish! I looked like, no, I *was* a departing princess, but minutes later, in the mirror of THE END, there was this girl facing me. This mousy, buck-toothed girl who – once upon a time – couldn't even afford ballet shoes. She looked me straight in the eye and said *Take them off*. The past started streaming down my cheeks, and as I stood barefoot in the puddle with a shoe in each hand, I finally, fully, understood that Happily-Ever-After is the beginning.

Upholstered Cumulus
Lucy Goldring

Stu had lost the coin toss. His back's spasming like it's fit to snap, and sweat is pouring down his arse crack – but helping to carry the spoils (*in this bastard fucking heat?*) was part of the deal.

If Mike's struggling up front, he's not showing it. His smooth, beige shoulders are unreadable.

They'd both had eyes for Danny – Danny Boy, Dan the Man – but Danny had only had eyes for assorted white powders. *Just chill the hell out, lads, yer?* he'd slur from the sofa as arguments flamed around him. While his body lay prone, his head got orbital, cruising laps of the pastel high-rises.

From the top of the road, Mike's new gaff shimmers into view. It mocks Stu with sunlit winks, shiny letterbox kisses – a pebbledash of screw you. The sight of it puts Red Bull in Mike's stride.

Stu's thinking he can't take much more; the sofa's thickening with the weight of Danny, with that last time. He pushes the image away, thinks instead of damp cement sacks, busted fridge-freezers, tall stacks of gold bullion – but it does him no good.

Crumbs and coins and toenail clippings bounce on the pavement as Stu drops his end of the sofa. He watches Mike stumble sideways in grit and piss and something like dead snail.

Fuck.

Mike is up, unbending to his full height, muscles thick with fury.

Stu fills his lungs, steadies his legs, braces himself for –

A clear plastic cylinder rattle-rolls towards the gutter.

Suspended in saline, Danny's eyes stare, seeing everything clearly for the first time. His friends stare back. *Shit*, they say in unison, *there's no escaping the bastard.*

The men set the sofa on its casters and take the weight off their limbs. They talk and they laugh and they cry like boys, until evening saps the colour from their cheeks, from everything that has gone before.

On their way back down, the sofa sheds its mass. A gentle breeze stirs and rises, swirling lazy eights between them, breathing kisses round their necks. *Keep it chill, lads, yer?* it murmurs – and Stu doesn't need to see Mike's face to know he's smiling too.

Spill
Rosaleen Lynch

A group of migrating jellyfish is called a smack

'I'm an immigrant, not ignorant,' Mama says to the man who calls her stupid and a filthy foreigner, shouting that we're all alike. She doesn't say she's a teacher and instead asks him to hold out his hands. Maybe she'll smack them like she does mine when she catches me with matches or I don't do what I'm told. He does what he's told. 'Other way,' she says. He turns them over, nails up, as she holds out her own. Hands hang in air, inches from the other, too high for me to see until he drops them with his eyes and his feet turn to go, hands filling his pockets with a curse.

Jellyfish are millions of years older than dinosaurs

Mama asks me, when we get home, as if we're in her classroom, with the papier-mâché planetary mobiles and faded window stickers of dinosaurs and jellyfish and burnt terracotta vases with our names lined up like soldiers on the windowsill, 'What's the lesson?' I don't know, I say, feet parallel to hearth, standing straight, hands at my side, nails facing out. Mama settles cup into saucer. One that when she's dead, I'll smash like an asteroid in the empty fire grate.

Jellyfish are ninety-five per cent water

Mama's waiting, but I can't answer how she wants. I listen. Let her fill me like a vase to full. But still, I don't heed the lesson about being cleaner, politer, and more careful than the next person. I travel, collect matchbooks everywhere I feel the spark of love. And I learn that sometimes it doesn't matter what you do; some people are so full of hate that all they can do is be cleaner, politer, and more careful when it spills.

Pasiphaë, the Wife of King Minos, Pays for His Meddling in the Business of the Gods
Jupiter Jones

Last spring, I heard it bellowing like a horn in the fog as it was unloaded at the quayside. Another sacrificial bull. Although he is king, my hubby is forever running errands for those Gods.

When the summer was blooming hot, pomegranates in season, courtyards suffused with their stink, lizards lounging in the cracks of the walls, I wandered the top fields seeking breeze, and that same bull was up there. Should've been ceremonially dispatched weeks since, but Minos had some foolish scheme. Grudgingly, I had to admit, this one was a handsome beast. A stud. I felt first a stirring in my groin, like a rag wrung, hitched up my skirts and climbed the fence. The bull, pawing dust, showed more irritation than interest. Bastard. I am queen, and what I fancy, I shall have.

I went to the workshops and demanded of that wizened old tinkerer Daedalus that he make me irresistible and mountable. He built a frame of steamed and bent timbers, a curvy arse-end, stretched over with tanned hide, dappled cream and brown. Suffocatingly hot and cumbersome too. Leather straps chaffed my thighs, but I wanted what I wanted. Daedalus stammered and faffed, offered to refine, line with silk, make fancy feathered ventilation worked by strings, but I wouldn't wait. Indeed, I could not.

Once was enough. Afterwards, the contraption was burned for the shame of it. I was sore and bled, so I thought no more.

That winter, the seas were calm for once. My belly swelled – with another young Minos – or I assumed. Well, isn't assumption the mother of all catastrophes? The Gods will have their sport, and in the cradle, my bellowing offspring wears a blue silk hood covering his bulging brow and scratch-mitts on his hooves. I'd pick him up, but already, he's too heavy. Three wet nurses have quit, their milk dried up, nipples in shreds. Minos weeps and renounces his insubordination. Daedalus is sketching a contrivance with pulleys and a flexible pipe to syphon from an udder, a set of bellows to draw suck. Mr Daedalus is quite the genius and not nearly as repellent as I first thought.

Things Beth's Mother Said About Angela Riley
Alison Wassell

Beth's mother had nothing against Angela Riley, but the family lowered the tone of the street with their shenanigans, and their noise, and the comings and goings of men at all hours of the night. The house was rented, not bought, and the rent was paid by the social. It made all the difference, said Beth's mother.

Angela Riley smelled as though she changed her knickers once a week, if she could be bothered. She scratched her scalp until it bled and wiped green candles from her nose with the sleeves of Beth's old cardigans because Beth's mother didn't like to think of the kiddie being cold.

Angela Riley played out with the big boys in the street long after Beth had gone to bed. She rattled the letterbox and ran away. She ripped petals from Beth's mother's tulips and ground them into the pavement with her filthy plimsoll, spitting words she should not have known when Beth's mother asked why she had done it. Beth's mother blamed the parents. Or the parent, to be more accurate.

Angela Riley got into trouble. It served her right, said Beth's mother, for playing with the bad boys. She flaunted her pregnant belly in a crop top, sitting on Beth's wall, tapping cigarette ash into the garden and singing 'Papa Don't Preach' at Beth's father when he shooed her away.

Angela Riley went into labour as Beth was sitting her first O level, and again the day she received her A level results.

'You and Angela are polar opposites,' said Beth's mother, waving her off to fulfil her potential, to return only rarely, and with her eyes on the clock, and her nose wrinkled with disdain. Angela Riley stayed, dragging up children, then grandchildren, fashioned in her own likeness.

Angela Riley came to Beth's father's funeral then back to the house for tea. She hugged Beth's mother fondly, almost like a daughter.

'He had a soft spot for you,' Beth's mother whispered.

Watching Angela Riley cross the road, Beth's mother turned to her with something approaching hatred in her eyes.

'Why couldn't you be more like her?' she said.

When the Trumpeter Carries On
Sherry Morris

Dad's wife Shirley calls. Invites me to Thanksgiving at theirs.

He's getting old she cajoles. *Misses you. He's your father, after all.*

Her nagging nasal voice whines down the line – an earworm I still don't know how to treat. My no-show at his big 7–0 hasn't been forgotten. I tell myself that like the times, he's changed. Tell Shirley, *Alright-alright, I'll go.*

Her expert speed-dial fingers deliver an impressive more-than-you-can-eat turkey-dressing-trimmings-pumpkin-pie buffet spread, but it's dread that fills my guts.

Everything is breezy-light – politely nice – until the overflow of afternoon drink spills into evening, and careful chit-chat fails. Dad sits, head of table, less than ruler-straight. His blood-orange face, puffed-out cheeks and twitching mouth are familiar yet distorted. The bulging eyes are new. I've been away a long, long time.

He starts. A variation of a tune I've been subjected to since childhood – subtle undertones and restrained melodies now morphed into bold, bombastic blasts.

We'll make America great again. Stop the steal. Deep State is real.

I sober fast watching this old man Trumpet live. It's somehow worse than his Facebook posts that belittle Black lives. He'll never change his bigot's tune. My tolerance of his intolerance has kept the peace. But I don't feel like peace right now. I want to make my own musical mark—

Crash cymbals either side of his head.

Bash a big bass drum to drown him out.

Take the bathroom plunger, cover and uncover his big blowhard mouth as he blares about building walls, that all goddamn lives matter, and I laugh and laugh as his -ists and -ics are wah-wahed away.

I take a deep breath. Interrupt. *Here's what I'm thankful for, Dad... You. I'm who I am because of you.*

In the silence, my words resonate. He'll hear them as he wants. What matters is I've said my truth. Regained my peace. I hum a tune, gather my things and leave.

Lend an Ear
Meredith Lynn Wadley

In a modern auditorium overlooking a copper-green alpine lake and boasting the finest acoustics, an elderly, armless nun from Macedonia, Land of Myths and Legends, settles on a gold-tasseled cushion centre stage. Her milky eyes gaze upon a full house, luxuriating in plush velvet seating.

A child-nun appears with a tattered red and green kilim case, which she sets before the armless nun.

With dexterous feet, the old nun opens the case and props a zurla upon a stand. She moistens the oboe cousin's reeds and seals its finger holes with her toes. A set of Macedonian folk classics, warbly high notes and enthralling trills, emerge in 22/16 timings.

Great applause.

The child nun reappears. 'It is not for woman to play zurla—' she says, her words accent-stilted.

'But as I am a virgin—' the old nun says.

Her grin is toothless.

A joke? The audience titters.

Following a set of modern homeland tunes and intermission, the nun plays a sassy set of pop interpretations in 7/8 timing: Michael Jackson's 'Black or White', Beyoncé's 'Pray You Catch Me', and Benjamin Clementine's 'Condolence'. Few in the audience recognise the tunes, but all jump to their feet as the nun retreats.

'Encore! Encore!' the audience cries, and the child nun returns.

'Mistress would shush you if she could.'

The audience murmurs.

'Mistress wishes each of you to lend her an ear.'

A puzzling request.

Several nuns pass baskets around, urging everyone to lend at least one ear.

As with any religious, charity, or busker's audience, some members worry about giving too much. Too little. Others determine to abstain, while still others flee their velvet seats.

The quality of each loaned ear discloses the quality of its owner: one gent worries about his ear's excessive hair; a young man frets that his may be cheesy; and a woman worries about the three-carat diamond stud in hers. The value of it could feed a Macedonian convent for months.

Arranged in an arc before the old nun, the ears on stage begin to glow, and the audience leans forward, each person fearful of difficulties hearing, being disabled as they are.

Permanent
Jamie D Stacey

They take the marker to you when you're in the womb, and you'll be born with *tattoos/ words/ the voices of everyone else*. The nurse will weigh you, the doctor will examine you, and before you've left the hospital there'll be more words along your arm: *boy/ underweight/ cries all the time*. You'll be surrounded by mum, no dad, and the rest of society. You'll learn to eat, sleep, walk and talk. You'll learn you're *nice/ naughty/ a difficult sleeper*. You'll learn families are natural disasters, schools teach discipline, not play, and you'll need to work hard to earn numbers written too close to your heart. You'll feel your lack of success. Lack of progress. Lack of girlfriends, indeed any friends. Too many zits. Too many ifs. Too much no. You'll let others write all over you, even the ones not there: *not tonight/ I'm busy/ I'm not your father I have no son*. You'll feel that familiar chisel tip, the feel of being freshly marked, and the feel of yesterday's faded marks that never truly leave. Sometimes, when days are wet and long and lonely, you'll take the marker, prick old words and recite them: *fickle/ failure/ fucked*. You'll do that, mark your entire body from head to heart except that one woman (there's always one) who'll wash you, bathe you, and when you're still messy and marked, she'll take her own pen and scribble poetry over pain. You'll learn what life could be, most of all, you'll learn to write *boy/ man/ someone who'll try his damned best to be a good father*.

And when it's your turn you will take that marker, you will mark your baby (because you will mark your baby), but you will make sure, at least, that the ink never dries on *love*.

Your Intemperate Life
Valerie Fox

Before you stopped believing in the God your parents feared, before you searched for your birth mother, before the heavy stick struck, before I was crouched by the snowy window and you said 'let's get married' over the phone, before you realized your mother (the one you had) could not make out the patterns of words and learned everything by rote, before you forgot to go to the promising job interview with the pharmaceutical-maker, before our last night of silence in your childhood home on the steep hill, before you understood that you had to turn your head like a bird so that your good eye could see straight, before the metal company, before the world got too small and possessed only you, before the mine your father worked closed down forever, before the path winding through stacks of newspapers in the attic, before twenty years worth of furry dust coated the framed picture of your last dog and, it's a good thing your mother did not live to find you there in her threadbare, gooseneck chair and we didn't have kids of our own.

Sing to Me of the Sea
Abigail Hennig

Some say it is the Hyades that bring the rain. She prays to them, just in case.

On the day the weather breaks, she stands at the window, gasping for a glimpse of sea. The sky shadows silver; unleashes a deluge as the child surfs and rolls inside her. With each swell, she breathes an intercession, for a baby who sings the ocean's tune.

For days it rains. People – eyes heavy and ash-bagged from the relentless hovering heat – peek from behind curtains, wait for clouds to disperse. Water makes them nervous. She does not understand.

The windows are small in the house of her hawk-eyed almost-husband. He watches her hold hands to her stomach, fingertips tracing ripples and waves, closes curtains tight.

For days it rains. Nights too, nights when she creeps outdoors to dance, hair matted, clothes sticky-backed to skin. Each time, he drags her indoors. Each time, she grows stronger.

On the third night, his fingers slide from her shoulders. With a last, helpless stare at the sky, he stumbles backwards, rewinding himself, climbs into his car and is gone, lost to empty, rainswept roads.

The baby stills.

Inside, she leans her body against a wooden trunk, rests her ear upon its lid to hear the whispery call of home. Creaking it open, she scoops the glistening robe from within, envelopes herself in silken threads, softness sinking into skin.

Outside, the weather wraps itself around her, twisting her hair into tendrils, running rivulets down her cheeks; it swirls oceans of water beneath her feet, urges her onwards, towards the shore.

There – two boundaries break.

She stands on a precipice as mucus and blood pool and she drowns in wetness as he slips through her legs, as she grapples to grasp his slimy, bawling body and then—

She holds him aloft.

Sighs a single word,

'Selkie,' as the rain finally stops; the sisterhood of stars fling sunlight across the water and she and her boy are embraced by the shimmering sea.

The River Thames' Secret Boyfriend
Barclay Rafferty

We holiday out of season.

Torquay in February; Cromer in December. Dog-walkers whistle, ask *why?* We like the way the water pleats in a high gale, we say, tosses hairstyles asunder. To hikers, we tell a different story. It's the snow-crush of wellies, the twee watercolours of post-box robins on the beachfront. We spend evenings squinting at the horizon, planning for next year, map splayed, fingers trysting past Paignton, Bodmin, across the Irish Sea.

The academic year ends, and we go our separate ways, home for summer. I go south, promise to return with thrifted pullovers and seconds-sale ceramics. My partner goes west, promises seashells – ghost boxes, she calls them – preserving the Atlantic's wheeze.

I lie to my father, tell him I'll be home for June, July at the latest. Promise.

You can't jump off Tower Bridge without making a splash, turning heads. So I paddle in on the Darent, breaststroke in chalk Downs, wade through frog skulls mauled by otters. My lover travels from the Cotswolds. 'Isis!' they yell. 'Isis!—'

Bankside, she talks of Caroline boys who coughed through summer plagues; of madmen who sailed at dusk – to Avon, Tamar, wherever, away from her. Old Father Thames has returned from sea, she says. He's reminiscing about pigs flying over Battersea; cannon blasts in Jacobean thatch; recusants in Gothic vaults. He and his daughter, he tells me, are three hundred and forty-six kilometres long, with an eighty-island kingdom, protected by MI5.

When I ask his permission, he tells me to leave, run, hide in Highgate Cemetery, skirt multi-storey car parks. In the safety of the Underground, he says, look up routes to St Ives, thumb iPhone notes about Manderley, Jamaica Inn.

And the answer is Never.

Michaelmas comes, and I ask my loved one if she fancies sharing a wet poke of chips in an A-frame tent along the Wild Atlantic Way. She says Yes, I do, I've spent many summers alone there. Then I ask her how beautiful Donegal is, how close to the ocean? And she just moulds her fingers to a conch shell and asks me to listen, to a song learnt in tiny streams, told to rivers, unrecognisable at sea.

Dalí's Moustache
Pedro Ponce

The ghost of Magritte watches two masked lovers kissing on a subway platform. In life, he was a painter, but in this moment, as he haunts the corners of the twenty-first century, Magritte has become a prophet. His disgust is profound. If he could access the physical plane of existence, he would tear at the nearest canvas with his palette knife or shatter blooms of wine and glass onto the walls of his studio. Instead, he can only hover impotently five centimeters over the gray pavement.

His fellow surrealists do what they can. It happens to the best of us, says the ghost of Dalí, who extends a consoling hand just shy of Magritte's overcoat. There's always next time, he adds, though the passing decades have yet to reveal whether reincarnation is still an option.

The ghost of Breton, roused from his nap, regards the graffiti phalluses on a nearby movie poster. It is better to be forgotten completely, he declares from his berth seven centimeters above the ground.

Magritte looks at Dalí, whose sympathy is never without a preening edge. Now imbued with the power of foresight, he delivers his next prophecy. One day, Dalí, you will be the realist.

Dalí's amused expression is unchanged as he sinks nearer to the pavement. But his moustache trembles like a pair of vigilant antennae, searching the air for passing feet.

With Time, Disintegration Will Pull the Layers Apart
June Drake

The small, beige floppy disk with the worn label was six years past its design life, but she pushed it into the salvaged drive anyway. *Worth a shot.* The machine hummed – quiet, steady, reliable – and opened the text files without so much as a groan.

In hindsight, it should have been a warning, how easy it was to strip off years of topsoil and expose her adolescent words to the air. A description, a curse, anything on the label might have waved off the incautious, made the file harder to open. Might have reminded her, before. *Before.*

She remembered his twin bed, the small bedroom with the door open. The pressure on her shoulders, pinning her.

Was that him, or was that the other one, later?

The assaults blended together sometimes, distinct forms pasted adjacent to each other, spelling something she hadn't worked out yet. *His mom walking by the bedroom with the laundry – was that intentional?* Back then, she'd chalked it up to luck, a random act that gave her a chance to run.

Still the words surprised her when she read them now. *Rapid, furious, sloppy.* She'd spat them. Scattered them. Buried them under cheap plastic and digital obsolescence.

On a cold stoop, she rang the bell, heard the muffled clusters of conversation. Exhaled. Forced the corners of her mouth upward. Raised her eyebrows to relax her eyes. Months of video calls had honed her muscle memory into Appropriately Cheerful But Not Too Much, an expression she had built carefully in all the years since he held her down. *You're allowed to feel anything as long as you're not too much.*

The door opened. Undercurrents of warm, spicy kitchen smells escaped and surrounded her.

'Hi, Mom.'

'Hi, honey. Glad you could make it.' Her mom gestured at someone in the living room. In the din. 'You remember Eric from down the street, right?'

Her mind hummed in the background. Steady. Reliable. She did remember him. Or the pressure of his hands on her shoulders, anyway.

She smiled. Appropriately. Almost too much, too much. *Too much.*

My Daughter Is a Fishing Net
Anne Howkins

Born a tangle of fibre knotted, knotted, knotted tight as a pearl-pregnant oyster.

I teased and puzzled at her until the unspooling agony drifted her away, hurt-balled to a sea urchin, wailing like electric wires slicing through the spin-drift, wanting only the ghost of her father.

When she was unravelled, she lay across me, crooning gently as her mesh and my flesh curled around each other. On her tantrum days, she origamed herself into a bundle weighted like a gillnet, casting onto my lap only at bath-time.

I gathered toys for her, glittery bright, to stalk and trap, tickling her fancy until she vibrated with something I hoped was delight. On quiet days, when the ghost of her father was away to the shore, she lay across my lap while I warped and wefted tinsel and ribbons, raffia, wool and rope into her sparkling mesh, stringing her with sea glass, mother of pearl and the shells I'd beach-combed when she was knotted floating in my womb.

Then the nights she rustled around the house, pushing against doors and windows, until she found a chink to octopus through, a high-tide line of trinkets dripping in her wake.

She brought home her catch. Unidentifiable rusted things. Drowned soft toys, their ears water-deafened to the wails of their children. Umbrella skeletons. Rodent skeletons. Purses and wallets with smudged photos of long-lost lovers. Keys to locks never to be re-opened. Lockets with hair that might be human. Decaying knives that might have been murder weapons. Corroded wedding rings, their engraved initials weeping brine. Objects of desire, objects of hatred.

When she'd done with her fishing, she folded herself tight, rocking gently to the susurrating shells woven to the heart of her – the augers, tellins, periwinkles, whispering tales of the lost at sea. Her answering moans were the rotting groynes calling for lost fishers, calling for lost loves, calling for lost fathers.

My daughter is a fishing net, cast adrift, trawling for a ghost, the vestiges of maternal love caught in the spaces between her threads.

Far from the City
Lee Hamblin

Far from the city, sound has room to breathe. Whispers and whooshes ebb and flow like ghostly map-in-hand pirates searching for treasure, dovetailed planks creak in the soft-swaying tilt of the left to right, and a man's falsetto lilts in the tide of moonshine. He hushes when it begins to rain and lulled to sleep by the pitter-patter on the tarpaulin above, dreams his dream.

A thunderclap cracks heaven, and a snow-white dagger pierces the ocean, but still the man sleeps. In his dream, he's weeping. He dreams the same dream; of a young girl with mousy hair and helpless eyes. His arms beckon her, and she comes close enough for him to feel her breath in his heart, then turns away, swallowed by a sea of tears.

He wakes, drinks straight from the bottle by his side, and raises a fist to the world. The storm has moved on, leaving behind a black sky and air whiffing of damp leather. In a while, he sleeps again, and when he opens his eyes at dawn, sees a cornflower-blue sky and hears the chirrup of tiny birds happy to have made it through the night. Aching empty and cold, he takes a piece of bread and a blanket from his holdall. He gazes at the majestic sun rising from the edge of the world, knowing he once believed in a god of sorts, wondering if he ever would again.

An old song comes to mind they used to sing on patrol. He hums the melody. A scruffbag of a dog on the quayside barks. He laughs; it's an awkward, forgotten pleasure that sounds strange for him to hear again. Another dog yelps, and suddenly there's a bark-off. It returns him to scrawny, desolate streets, to an unforgiving sun, dust, and the cacophony of silence.

The man puts on his damp boots, splashes his face with seawater, and salutes a thank you to last night's borrowed lodgings. His holdall weighs heavy on his shoulder, so he adjusts the straps until it sits a little easier. He stands tall, takes a deep breath, and heads back towards the city.

She Follows a Familiar Recipe
Emma Louise Gill

I lay ingredients on the granite bench: buttermilk, flour, baking soda. Rosemary snipped last night under the full moon. Salt distilled from the ocean, the way you taught me. Honey from the beehive I placed in your wildflower meadow. The blooms are divine this time of year, while azalea and oleander creep in, poison sweet.

Next I pre-heat the oven, combine these memory-fruits, soft and doughy in dry hands that crack like your temper, your tepid-water brain. My knuckles are swollen, veins protruding. You always said the rheumatoid would get me first, wise women though we are. Another petty prediction proven true. I push into my floured surface anyway, pull and spread, tug and squeeze. My shoulders insist they're growing old, but I resist their surrender. Your parchment scrawls lead the way.

Sunrise casts her golden glow into the kitchen. The starlings are awake and warbling. If I can't lubricate my joints with this – the joy of purpose, the doing of wise work – I don't deserve your legacy. Whether I want it is another matter.

I form a heart-shaped fold – whether for you or me, it isn't clear – then into a round, scored thrice. The oven beckons. Its door is broken, hooked closed, yet still the warmth escapes. You said I could not replace it 'til you were dead and gone. It reminds me always of you.

Now, an hour of peace. My favourite time of day. I sit with tea and feed the starlings, watching clouds gather in the sky. When the garden turns silent and still, I head indoors. The bread is done, and all the house knows whom it's going to. I wrap the cooling loaf in spider-silk and muttered charms.

Half-dead lilies on your windowsill splice the air with perfume. I replace them, ready for the day I cast them on your grave. Rheumy grey eyes, once razor-sharp, follow me, but you don't say a word until my gift is revealed. Then you rip your taloned nails into the loaf and smile.

'Just like my daughter used to make,' you say.

I nod and wait for the honey to complete my work.

Elizabeth – Room Number 2
Rachel Canwell

When they hand in the room keys, the receptionist looks away. Mutters something about the weather and then busies herself with all the brightly coloured leaflets on the stand.

They head out to the prom and walk along, his hand tightening around her waist, a little more insistent with each step. He pauses every so often to land occasional wet kisses on her carefully made-up cheek. His breath is hot, loaded with stale alcohol, fried food and that familiar sour odour of apology and shame. The normal balm for day-old bruises.

Elizabeth stares straight ahead and tries to make herself part of the noise, part of the blue sky and the candy-flossed expectation of this perfect summer's day.

She is so focused on just being that she can't remember how they get to The Hall of Mirrors.

But here they are.

And here she stands. And stares. Facing now after row of distortion. Row after row of lies.

Ten Elizabeths. All standing in a line. Ten broken women, each with the same haunted expression, each with questioning eyes.

Until Elizabeth at the back winks.

And inclines her head towards the neon exit sign.

The Truth About Mountains
Abbie Barker

In the sag of midlife, you wanted to know mountains. Not their names or elevations, but how they felt. You planned to claim every peak in the state. I asked how long you needed. You squinted as if you didn't understand the question.

That fall, we hiked Kearsarge with our epileptic dog, the valley engulfed in flame-colored leaves. I kept saying how beautiful it was, how stunning. It was then you told me there are two types of people: those who hike for a view and those who hike for more. I said, yes, some chase the destination, others the journey. You shook your head, like no, that wasn't it at all.

After that, I stopped going. Or you stopped asking. Your trips stretched over days and weekends, then weeks. The dog had three seizures in one day. You weren't here when I put her down. You weren't here when I got the call from my mother. You weren't here.

I stopped sleeping. The doctor blamed hormones – not a spike, but a waning. I changed my diet and slept late, then later. You tried dragging me out of bed one morning as if you knew the cure. You said, come with me, up Mt. Washington. I pulled away, saying you already did that one. Not in the snow, you told me, not in the snow.

You think truth is found on mountains. Not at the summit but along the trail. Maybe you feel it in a breath or a dripping bead of sweat. Maybe you see it in a luminous flash skittering across the snow. These are only guesses. The way I see it, there are two types of people. Those who lock ourselves in, and those who leave and leave and leave, each time returning with less.

Seed Money
Sara Hills

For only seventy-seven dollars, the TV preacher promises God will grant me a miracle. He clasps his hands in prayer, gold rings glinting, while I clasp the telephone, punching the numbers from the TV screen that casts the room in a greenish glow.

'There, there,' the woman in the phone says, shushing me, and already I feel the miracle of Mama refilling my cracks.

The woman waits while I tiptoe through our dark trailer, careful not to step on the stain, careful not to disturb the steady rasp of Daddy's sleep-breathing or his one arm hanging off the bed. I find his jeans in the empty dent on Mama's mattress side and slide the V-I-S-A card from his torn leather wallet.

Stretching the phone to the dawn-lit window, I whisper the bumpy numbers, which the woman makes me do twice, asking how old I am (seven), asking if I have any pets (yes, a dog: Roy), asking if I ever planted beans at school (not at school, with Mama), and did I know beans are seeds and seeds grow miracles? And the more seed money we plant, the more miracles God can bring to the world?

I sink down against the wall, burying my fingers into the knotted fur along Roy's ridges where the fat ticks hide, while the woman on the phone calls me honey and God's little angel.

Her voice hums, like bees waking in springtime or when the neighbor's cat Carlo catches a mouse. Her voice hums, and it's like Mama's kneeling there next to me, fingernails heavy with dark dirt. Only this time, Daddy's not shouting, and Roy and I aren't whimpering; it's just the woman's voice filling my belly with dollar amounts and seed names – Resurrection, Recovery, New Beginning – so soft and sure they feel like an already answered prayer.

Roof of Hope
Carrie Beckwith

Delhi heat is like a blanket laid over your head. Not a light blanket with air holes but an old blanket, a thick one, like what you'd put over a horse, heavy and stodgy like a canvas mattress stuffed with straw. In those cramped weaving alleys, people moved about their business slowly.

And these alleys were our playground; me and my sister playing tag before sunrise, her face a rash of blisters from the heat and dust. My grandmother watching over us slowly, dabbing her chin with her cotton dupatta as she'd tell me to bring the water, child. And the heat settling in heavier at night, making our beds up on the roof, my grandmother sponging our restless bodies with a cold rag and blowing on our naked chest and bellies. And worse still when the Loo wind blew, and she'd herd us all inside from its hot dry breath. Saving us from the prickles, aches and dizziness, but the house like an oven, giving us a thirst no guzzling could quench.

'It's getting hotter, Santosh,' she said to my father. 'There must be something we can do?'

When the lady came, grandmother took her inside and up to the roof, and she walked around tapping her phone and said, 'You will need four.' Days later, she returned in a tuk-tuk with four big pots of white paint. My father scratched his head but agreed when grandmother gave him one of her looks. I watched him paint from a shaded corner, the white carpet creeping closer until I stood on the last dark spot.

'Now where you going to go, Poonam?' He laughed, swinging me onto his shoulders.

That night we took our pillows up and slept without a care. The white paint 'a miracle' my grandmother praised God for. It pushed the heat away, you see, as the lady had said, reflecting the heat, not absorbing it. Even inside was cooler, and some days, I could take a nap, falling asleep to the whirring of the fan blades above.

The alleys are still sweaty, though, but perhaps we could paint those as well?

Colouring Outside the Lines
Sharon J Clark

The giraffe was discovered on the wall of the motorway underpass on a damp day in mid-October. The place was a favourite haunt of teenagers from the high school. They'd laid claim to the space with spray-painted tag names and crudely drawn genitalia. The life-size giraffe with its bold chestnut patches was a shock of beauty amongst the ugliness.

A week later, it was joined by an African elephant, ears wide and erect, trunk raised in exaltation. No one questioned its ownership of the space. It was majestic, awe-inspiring, utterly splendid.

Then came a tiger with golden eyes and a wise expression. Soon after this, the trio was joined by a richly tusked warthog and a murder of crows. Nobody knew who was transforming this dank hideout for youngsters wanting to rebel with cigarettes and cheap booze. Not Banksy, for sure. This wasn't his style.

Families started to visit at weekends. When December arrived, someone strung sets of fairy lights high in the concrete buttresses. On Sundays, a mobile coffee van parked on the nearby road, tempting visitors to cinder toffee lattes and butter-rich pastries. More animals appeared, and during the week, childminders brought their little ones for wintry picnics, saying it was educational.

Two months later, the image of an ark materialised on the last remaining concrete space. It was open-doored with an entry plank painted across the dirty tarmac path. The local news programme sent a reporter and cameras. Someone asked about the source of the electricity for the fairy lights. No one knew the answer to that.

Then, one frosty day in February, it was gone. The ark, the animals, the lights – nothing remained except a wash of sea-green paint covering every surface. Someone said it was the town council. Someone else blamed the local neighbourhood watch, who were tired of the crowds and people peeing in their gardens. Someone said the animals had sailed away in the ark.

The high school kids returned. The fags and the booze and the outlines of penises too. And somewhere in the dark of a cold spring night, an artist sighed and moved on.

Searching for Sun in the Sunflowers
Kate Simblet

I open one eye, smell daffodils. A fanfare of trumpets waves from the juice jug, you smile from a plastic chair. Blue, our backdrop of cubicle curtains – we're together in a room with no view. You prattle along as if words alone can cure my mood, but they drift like blossom to the floor. Spring's sprung, apparently. Bulbs, last year planted, have bloomed, transforming your garden into a vivid palette. There's snowdrops, irises, narcissi.

My colours are muted, but I see the black dog. Like a shadow, he's stalked me since he found me years ago, lately dead-weighting my chest. Faithful, unshakeable, he refuses to leave, so they've ordered me here to find 'rest'. I'm sad – too lethargic to get down on all fours, creep past the nurses, sneak through locked doors down endless mopped corridors to find a way out. But if I could lose this dog and follow my heart, might I burrow and exit in the peace of a forest? Luxuriate, flat-foxed on a soft bed of moss, draw in the oxygen I crave. I lie here marooned in bluey-dark depths, now bleach is the only smell. The scent of your daffodils robbed by the hospital. You tell me to keep on taking the pills. That dog keeps on stealing my breath.

~

Three sunflowers wearing cellophane lean like bored teenagers against wipe-clean magnolia. The freckles on your arms spell out its summer, but this season always leaves me cold. You complain it's too stuffy – that there's no time to garden, that visits swallow your weekends.

I remember planting sunflowers when we were kids – the wait for tiny leaves, unfurling, splitting seeds. Pots side by side, on the same windowsill, each one a promise that things do grow and change. Our grandma on a mission at planting out time, evaporating slugs with her teaspoons of salt. She claimed it didn't hurt, but we'd learned how adults lie. Seeds turned to seedlings, becoming plants, pole-tied. Always a lottery which ones would survive the perils of harsh weather, animals, snails – or the monster that visited at night. Yours always seemed to grow taller and stronger. Somehow, yours always thrived.

Sculptress
Anne Daly

I take a walk each morning with my son. His fingers, warm as treacle, curve into my hand as we step through the orchard. In spring, the trees arch and trail confetti blossoms across the stippling breeze. His apple cheeks puff and blush with pride when he runs in front of me, his little bones unsteady in their movements as if held together by the most delicate of threads.

We pass his father's studio and peep through the high arching windows. The light is dizzying, how it reflects off the white walls and bursts into feathers against the dust-addled air. Sometimes he is at work, bent over a block, smoothing sinew with his rasp, the bone-coloured marble warming beneath his touch. He pours life into its lines, effortlessly creating movement from stone.

She is often there too, of course. His apprentice. Her onyx curls pinned back, her pretty form swamped in overalls, plaster kissed. Her eyes are haughty and cold except when he speaks to her in that language of angles and arcs that they share.

Today the studio is empty. I leave my little one playing with daisies and step inside. There are tools and plaster limbs strewn all over the floor. In one corner, a figure crouches, its proud head emerging, mouth agape, as if amazed to find its body entombed in stone. On a pedestal, two dancers are awash in waves of bronze.

I walk over to her workspace, a wooden table splattered with paint. On it, an unfinished marble, the head and fragile shoulders of a little girl. Her hair and snub nose are captured perfectly, but the eyes are too opaque. The opalescence of the pupils gives a knowing air, too indifferent to be truly those of a child. I smile coldly and flick my wrist at it with distaste. He will not admire it.

The heavy door swings behind me. I return to my boy, scoop him up in my arms, spill pure joy as he sails towards me. Laughter sings the pattern of his pulse on my skin, the billow of his blonde curls becoming my horizon.

Silver Washed Fritillary
Sarah Bailey

(Rare orange and black patterned butterfly, silver under its wings.)

I lie at a distance from them, shaded in the hedgerow. Wild violets spread across the woodland floor, their bishop's purple shaking in the welcome breeze. The breath of air moves through my damp shirt as my elbows press into the dry soil, bearing the weight of the camera. With a somewhat desperate desire, I hunt the silver washed fritillary.

My hope, for footage of them feeding, has almost died. Just yesterday, I saw two duelling in the high trees. But today, they are elusive, wary of being pinned by the camera, as their predecessors are skewered, down the road, in the Littlehampton Museum.

The presence of my son on the other side of the hedgerow is heavy and distracting. I can just see his arm through the hawthorn, propping his flop of hair over the phone. Suspended, again, from school, I bring him or risk the alternatives.

He bears my broad brow, wide-set eyes – I understand the surface but can't get in.

A kind, 'How are you doing?' met with a barely audible, 'Fine'.

Defensive dark shadows cover him, but I know there is a wash of silver underneath – a lightness I have not seen for so long.

In despair of the sighting, I swing my camera up, resting momentarily on my back, panning across the blank, sky void. Rolling again, the camera aims out through the green spikes, and I capture my son heading away across the stubble. Heeding his own desire line, his arms are raised as if dancing, talking, flying, guiding in a plane or reckoning with God – I don't know. His stone washed, ripped, T-shirt rises up above his jeans, exposing a flash of pale vulnerability.

The Ghost in My Machine
Adele Evershed

I read a story online about an ordinary man – his dead girlfriend kept contacting him on Facebook. Through the mush and the static, she appeared sitting or standing in photos where she would've been if she weren't dead. He saw her laughing behind a mask at Halloween, or the back of her head in a concert crowd.

When I was young, I believed behind the finch's song, the voices of the dead were calling my name, and so it made sense to look for you in all the white noise.

The Egyptian's wrote letters to their recently departed in bowls – begging for help with the insoluble problems of living. And in Mexico, they built altars – *altares de Muertos* – to welcome the spirits. So I ordered a set of three mini teak alters from Etsy and set up a shrine. I arranged the photo of us on a rocky beach in Malta, your lighter engraved with a bee that you nervously flicked before you asked me to marry you. Next, I weigh down a sliver of your favorite sweater with your lucky stone that you found on a camping trip when you were young. I'd laugh when I found it at the bottom of the washing machine because you'd left it in a pocket. And of course, you didn't have it with you that day. In the paper bowl, I wrote, 'I'm sorry. I'm waiting for you,' and I filled it with bright marigolds.

But the flowers turned brown, and I found out the dead girlfriend story was just a well-crafted spooky tale posted on Reddit. Your ghost began to shrink to a shadow in a selfie or a whisper on a windy night. Or maybe I'd lost my desire to be haunted.

I know someday, we will all be ghosts, fragments of memory on a device; if they want to hear the voices of the dead, they'll sit around a campfire and just press play. Standing in the rain shadow now, feeling blurry at the edges, I listen to your voice mail – wavery, so you even sound like a spirit. 'Call me back when you get this.'

As Quiet As a Mouse
Denny Jace

'The kitchen.' The agent presents the room with a thespian's flourish. The rusted tap, long past its final drip, has eroded wounds inside the Belfast sink. Behind it, the windowsill holds a scattering of tiny black flies, snared in a feast of grease. Wall units hang open, having taken their final breath, detached from the walls, their weight tilting them precariously towards floor. Drawers, open and empty, house spiders in spongy webs.

'The office tells me you're new to the area, Ms Reynolds.' He pauses, his eyes sweeping the room, seeking inspiration.

'No,' I say, 'I'm not new. I'm moving back.'

'Oh. Okay.' I watch a shadow of worry flatten out his features.

'Are you familiar with the history of the house?' He asks.

'No,' I say. The lie burning my mouth. 'Mind if I look myself?' I add, pushing past him.

The stairs are bleached at the sides of each step where a carpet runner once lay. I stretch my leg up to the third step, the silent one that doesn't belie the night creeper. My hand clutches the bannister; I remember the feel of wood against my stomach, friction halting the slider's speed. *There were good times.*

On the landing, time has stolen space. The bones of the walls bend in on themselves, the ceiling hunchbacked. The room on the left has the door ajar. As I push through, its hinges groan with grief.

The cardboard at the window has come away like a torn flap of skin. Daylight sneaks in and stripes the wooden floor. Loose chunks of plaster hang from the walls, stuck with the print of swaying poppies, damp and faded.

Hello, I whisper, *I promised I'd come back.*

Beneath the silence, I hear your tiny lungs gasping for air, suffocating you. Born too soon, you ripped and tore me. I held you tight as your body stilled and your sticky skin turned cold. In the corner is the cupboard where they found you. Empty now, the door torn from its hinges. I'd wrapped you in my T-shirt, and there you lived, as quiet as a mouse.

Field Trip
Rebecca Shahoud

You zoom in, forefinger and thumb squeezing, pinching, pressing, clicking. You spin past the Walvis Bay and Tmassah and Trava. You want to go to Trava. Up, past mossy tendrils, icy capillaries, thin yellow scars, the green gouged out to make way for blue, the Channel, the home counties, the rows of grey bones and teeth. You are in one of those teeth. Forefinger, middle finger, squeeze tighter, grasping. Pixels fraction into something clearer. Green and grey blobs. Blobs become Lego trees, the heath, bathing ponds. You once snuck in at night to swim deep, cold, both of you, safe.

Your wife makes you mad, doesn't she? She confiscated your camera.
You can't use it anymore. It's your livelihood, thrown at the wall. Why? What are we going to do?
You're too young for this shit.
The walls are painted yellow.
Can you tell me what day it is, what month? Do you remember coming here?
Memories. Some you can, others you can't.
You were taken by a man in a blue suit then rolled into an MRI doughnut.

You zoom out, then back into varicose rivulets, dosette box fields, swathes of green nothing. Guangdong, Guangzhou, Zhaoqing. You recognise the name, you search. Did you film there once? Chillies, star anise. They don't serve that in this place.

You look up. She's in the doorway, smiling this time. Visiting hour.
You're safer here. It's Thursday. Art therapy. Will you? You can come back to your world afterwards.
You go. They are all older than you, stiller, slower. A woman gazes past you, the milky hollows of cataracts. She has lost a slipper. You hold a paintbrush in your hand, poised to paint that animal, that animal with hooves.
You were good, better. You want them to know that.

Ova Ovoid Ovate Ovum
Martha Lane

Omelettes
Scrambled.
Fried. Boiled. Poached.
Monday.
Tuesday.
Wednesday. Thursday. Friday.
Weekends, you coddle.

It started with breakfasts. Lunch, and then dinners. You can't remember precisely, or even vaguely, when you stopped eating anything else. In the evenings, you paw your silken clutch, counting, terrified you'll wake hungry. You scribble a hurried note – thirty, any size, free-range – in case. In case you knock one off the counter, or they rot when left untended. In case they simply disappear.

Exhausted from flitting down the staircase seven, eight, nine times a night – you roost in the kitchen, dizzy with visions of yolks oozing.

Shattered shells spill from the bin, feed you dreams of building nests.

You shred paper, but it slices. You bleed.

You gather moss, but it seeps. Reeks of mushroom gills.

You spin sugar, but it burns. Rotten candyfloss billowing.

You lose all your money on pans after you lose all your fingertips to soap suds. Hot water shifting more skin than scorch. But you learn. You learn the exact ochre at every centigrade. The clockwise swirl. The whip of the wrist until it's natural, like breathing. Like weeping.

Spoon handles jut from every surface as the sugar dries in sucrose stalactites. Your home, a steel jaw. A trap. Its teeth feathered with honey threads. You, the fox.

Egg-wrecker.

It's not your fault; it's innate. So, you build your guards of toffee twigs. Demerara defences. Sweet and cloying, protecting the eggs as your hollow belly rumbles. Sugar seeds litter the floor, crunch beneath you and fix you. Stuck, you weave treacle webs into the walls.

Eggs intact, unhatched.

Remember, it's not your fault.

Breathing molasses, you embrace your caramel cage.

On a Quiet Sunday Morning
Iva Bezinovic-Haydon

She'll read the story on a quiet Sunday morning in her pyjamas, a cup of coffee in her hand. Then she'll put the laptop you got her for her birthday down on the kitchen counter and say: 'Listen to this.'

You usually appreciate her enthusiasm to share the stories she enjoys, but on that Sunday morning, your mind will be somewhere else. You'll be worried. About the bite underneath your collarbone, about the smell of sex in your car, about the notes you keep finding in your pockets. You'll be angry at yourself. How on Earth did you ever get involved with a student? Last night was definitely the last time.

Your fiancée will start reading the story out loud, slightly rushed with excitement, swallowing some of the syllables. You'll find her energy overwhelming and suffocating. You'll want to snap: 'Please, can't you see I'm doing something else?' but you won't want to give away that you're irritable.

Upon hearing the first few sentences of the story, you'll stop with the useless task of pouring cereal from a cardboard box into a plastic container. You'll rush to say: 'Wait, slow down a bit,' scared of missing a word and immediately annoyed that your own words silenced those being read. You'll carefully put everything down on the wooden work surface, you'll focus. You'll freeze. A pause, a deep breath, and you'll ask in what you're hoping is a calm voice: 'Who wrote this?' even though you'll already know. You'll stand in your kitchen, your fists and stomach clenched, and you'll listen to your fiancée say the name you swore you never wanted to hear again.

Clueless of the change in you, she'll lift her slender arms above her head and stretch: 'It's great, right? So much raw pain and hurt, described so effortlessly. I wish I could write like that.'

You'll respond, maybe a bit too hastily: 'You're so much better than her.'

She'll jokingly squint at you. She'll know you're lying, but on that quiet Sunday morning, when your perfect fiancée reads you my imperfect story about us, you'll pray she doesn't know what you're lying about.

REFLEX PRESS

Reflex Press is an independent publisher based in Abingdon, Oxfordshire, committed to publishing bold and innovative books by emerging authors from across the UK and beyond.

Since our inception in 2018, we have published award-winning short story collections, flash fiction anthologies, and novella-length fiction.

www.reflex.press
@reflexfiction